SOMETHING AKIN TO REVULSION

Copyright © 2022 Judith Sonnet

ISBN: 9798846904057

All Rights Reserved

Printed in the USA / August 17th, 2022.

Cover design by Christy Aldridge

The events, characters, and locations in this book are all fictional. Any resemblance to reality is unintended and coincidental.

TRIGGER WARNING: None of these stories are good for your health. They all contain graphic depictions of violence, abuse, and bad behavior. Do not read this collection if you are easily offended.

CONTACT JUDITH SONNET AT:

Instagram: Fulltimehorrorjunkie

Twitter: JudithSonnet

Facebook: Judith Sonnet

Also by Judith Sonnet:

We Have Summoned

Cabin Possessions

Repugnant

For the Sake Of

For the Sake Of (2)

Torture the Sinners!

The Clown Hunt

Greta's Fruitcup

Your God Can't Save You

Chainsaw Hooker

For

Everyone in the Audience

SOMETHING

AKIN

TO

REVULSION

A Collection of Nasty Stories

By

Judith Sonnet

CONTENTS:

LOLCOW

LIQUID SICK

REHEARSAL

BODY-CRUNCH

COKE-NAIL

SOMETHING AKIN TO REVULSION

AFTERWORD (STORY NOTES)

SOMETHING AKIN TO REVULSION

LOLCOW

I like to edit and re-release clips from the most humiliating videos I can find on the internet. It's just a hobby to me... or it was until I was introduced to Rufus.

I was sort of frustrated. I had been doing this for a year, and all I had essentially accomplished was nothing. I wanted to feel like a journalist does when they break in on a coverup. So, I went to reddit and asked if anyone could help me find an up-and-coming LolCow.

"LolCow" means: a person that can be milked for laughs, often without their consent.

Very quickly, I was DM'd from an account that looked like a burner. They sent me a video file with the title: "Rufus Loves His Momma". I clicked on the video:

Rufus was nude. He was ugly too. Warty and pasty and his underarms were so hairy it looked like he had crammed oily mopheads beneath them. His face sheened with grease and his lips were so pink they looked like raw ham. He was unwashed. Even from the shitty video I could tell that he had patches of fuzzy mold growing in abundance beneath his flaps. And his naval? I'd never seen anything like it. It was crammed with gunk and fluffy bits of fungus. He had a row of pimples leading down the middle of his chest. Huge, white, and hard. They looked like their cream had solidified into a custard.

His penis looked like a fruit-roll up. It was a deep purple; tightly compacted with unwashed skin and dripping with grey snot.

He was holding a soiled diaper out so that the audience could see its gummy contents. The fecal matter inside the padded garment was absolutely diseased. Brown and syrupy all at once. It was congealed in the middle where black strips of indigestible food lay in an almost symmetrical tread. It reminds me of seaweed floating in a mud puddle.

"I'm gunner do it." It sounded like he was threatening suicide.

"Rufus, don't you dare!" A voice rose from behind the camera.

"Imma do it, mama!"

"Rufus, if you eat that thing, I'll whup ya good!"

I started to laugh. The dynamic between the two was perfect.

He began to eat the contents of the diaper. He shoveled strands of fibrous material into his gullet and snuffled piggishly. He didn't seem to care that iced-tea-colored liquids were slipping down his chin and dotting his pimple-mounted chest.

"Oh, Rufus!" His mamma screamed, as if she was being railed by her own son. "Oh, yer gonna get now!"

Then, a terrible thing happened. After licking up the contents of the diaper, Rufus picked up the camera and shuffled it around.

"Whath-chu gunner do, huh? What-chu gunner do 'bout it, Mar-ma!?"

The camera refocused and I felt my laughter die in my throat.

Rufus's Mama was a quadruple amputee.

She was ancient too. Her skin was grey and tattered. Fat bruises and lumps grew beneath the stumps where her limbs had once sat. There had been nothing clean about her amputations. The holes were sloppily sewed up. They looked like black mouths with whiskered stitching's. The seal on her left leg-stump had broken and the hole was leaking a black liquid that reminded me of beans breaking through a soft taco.

She was nude too. Her vagina was inflamed with infection. A gummy film grew over its slit. I imagined the flesh tearing if she tried to pry her cunt-flaps open. How did she even pee out of that thing? Or was the piss building up behind the seal like a literal "beaver dam"? Would one wrong move cause a geyser of week-old, stagnant urine to cascade from her and stream across the sofa she had been laid upon?

I clicked away from the screen and decided to watch some *My Little Pony* to relax.

The next day, another burner account sent me a new collection of videos.

I wish I could tell you why I watched them all. Maybe it was morbid curiosity.

He pried her cunt open, put an inflatable rubber ball in it, and blew it up so her vagina looked like a mound of creaking flesh. When he pulled the ball out, it came free with a wet pop that left her vagina hanging like a sleeve.

He brought in a German Shepard and let it hump her through her shit-crusted rear. She cried while the dog thumped its red-rocket in-and-out of her traction-less anus. After it came, Rufus threw the dog aside so he could capture the dribbles on camera.

He put an O-ring gag in her mouth and poured the dog's blood into it. I don't know when or how he killed the dog, but I know it's dead because he's wearing the dog's head like a demonic strap-on. His purple cock was sticking through the dog's hollowed head and out of its snout like a bloated tongue. His cockhead is beaded with creamy cum. The milky whites contrast the dark reds almost beautifully.

Each video was terrible, but the last one was different...

Rufus looked into the camera and said: "So, whaddya think o' my LolCow?" He slapped his mama's sallow belly. "She'th pretty good but... she's about out. I'll need a new 'un soon."

The image cut to black. When it came back the shaky footage was right outside my house.

He had left a package on my doorstep.

You probably already know what was in it. Of course, he had added his own twist to the horror of opening the brown package and revealing his mama's decapitated head. He had filled a sandwich bag with cum and stuffed it into her toothless mouth.

When I came back into my room, I saw another message in my inbox. It was titled: "NEW LOLCOW". Beneath it, there was a picture of my mother.

"Why?" I wrote.

Rufus responded: "Cuz it's funny."

SOMETHING AKIN TO REVULSION

LIQUID SICK

Jennifer didn't think twice before sending her vitriolic post into the ether. She didn't think about the people that it would hurt, or the people that would be encouraged to hurt over it. Instead, she simply smiled to herself for a job well done. The post was headlined by a news article. It read: "Trans woman found beaten near-death in public restroom". Jennifer wrote: "As far as I'm concerned, HE got what HE deserved. Was probably a pervert. #keepmenoutofourbathrooms". She sent the post, and it was immediately liked by her friends. They all agreed with her. Jennifer's social media presence was an echo-chamber, where she felt safe amongst likeminded women. Or, as she thought of them, *real* women.

"Mom." Ryan looked up from his phone. They were sitting across from each other at the dinner table. A hot breakfast had been eaten and Ryan's father was already out the door and headed to work. Jennifer and Ryan tended not to talk when they were alone in the house, as they often found themselves disagreeing.

Jennifer insisted she was a liberal, but she thought Ryan was taking things "too far". Her son was *basically* a socialist. With his painted fingernails and eye shadow, she often worried that he was being groomed by the LGBTQ crowd... but she had investigated his computer and was thankful to find straight pornography in his search history. Not that she had any real issue with gays and lesbians. She just didn't agree with the gender-switch-a-roo that was overtaking society. Like a lot of things Jennifer disagreed with, she considered it taking a step "too far".

"What is it, son?" She said and looked up from her phone. Jennifer was tall, wore her brown hair long, and always dressed elegantly. Even in the safety and comfort of her home, she wore a fashionable blouse and tight jeans. She was in her forties but looked to have just turned thirty-three. Her eyes were graced with stern crow's feet.

"Did you... did you mean to post this?" Ryan turned his phone around. She saw the article she had just shared and her caption.

"I did."

"Mom... that woman is in a coma. She's—"

"He." She interjected. "Just because 'HE' wears a dress doesn't mean we have to call 'HIM' by 'HIS' made-up pronouns."

"Mom." Ryan sounded exhausted. Older than his sixteen years. He furrowed his brow and sighed. "Mom that's not fair. Who is she—?"

"*He.*"

"Who is she hurting by being herself?"

"For one, he's hurting himself. If God wanted him to have a vagina, He would have given him one. This unstable man going to look back on his silly outfits and be so embarrassed when he's older."

"Mom. That's not true. Very few people regret transitioning—"

"And for another, he's putting a lot of *real* women in danger by entering their private spaces. What if the person that beat him up was a mother defending her little girl from a pervert? What if he was just in there trying to peek in on—?"

"Trans women aren't doing that. They're in more danger in public space than cis women right now, Mom. You're being unfair."

"I'm a feminist." Jennifer said. "And I want to protect w*omen* from *men* like this." She pointed at the article on Ryan's phone. "This creep deserved what he got."

It didn't sound like venom to Jennifer. It didn't sound hateful or cruel. To Jennifer, she was simply being logical. She beamed as her defeated son looked back at his phone and sighed. He turned back toward his breakfast and began to eat languidly, knowing that he couldn't argue with him mother.

It was like talking to a brick wall.

Jennifer hadn't bothered to read the article. If she had, she would have known that the assailant had already been caught. It was a man that had followed the trans woman –a woman named Kellie Roth—into the bathroom and had beaten her to a pulp simply for existing. Simply for having to pee and needing a receptacle.

If Jennifer had actually *read* the article, she would have learned that the assailant had ties to a neo-Nazi group, and that he had also been arrested for assaulting a Black man in a subway car two years prior. But in Jennifer's eyes, the assailant was a caring mother and a hero. A vigilante that was keeping bathrooms safe... safe for "real" women. In Jennifer's eyes, she would have done the same thing if presented with the right opportunity.

Jennifer looked at her phone and saw that one of her buddies had left a comment. It read: "AMEN".

Jennifer beamed, proud to be supported.

Ryan stood and brought his dishes to the sink. He said nothing. A cloud hung over his head.

Jennifer watched him out of the corner of her eye, knowing that he disapproved of her views. She knew he'd understand when he got older and had kids of his own. She knew he'd do anything to keep them safe. Especially if they were girls.

Jennifer though that the world could be so cruel to girls.

She put her own soiled dishes next to Ryan's —she would clean them later—Jennifer walked upstairs and went to the bathroom. After brushing her teeth and flossing, her stomach grumbled. She sat on the toilet and sighed as she released a few pebbles of scat. Like the rest of her life, even her bowel movements tended to be neat and organized. She closed the lid so she wouldn't have to look at her mess and pressed the lever. Nothing happened. The toilet gurgled but refused to flush.

Great. She sighed and rolled her eyes. She pressed down on the handle again, hoping it had been a fluke and that the toilet would roar to life. Alas, her stool was left in the basin.

As if the pipes had realized what they had been consuming all these years and now refused to swallow another brown bite.

Whatever. I'll call a plumber if Matt can't fix it. She wished her husband wasn't always so quick to leave the house. She'd have to text him and let him know the upstairs toilet wasn't working. She'd rather he fix it than a stranger.

Leaving her scat unflushed, she washed her hands and left the bathroom. By then, her phone was pinging with activity. Her gal-pals wanted to meet up for coffee and brunch today and one of them had started a group chat so they could get organized.

Having forgotten about the disobedient toilet, she joined in the conversation.

†

Two days passed before Jennifer got sick.

In that time, she had made more posts on her social media page about multiple important issues. She shared support for a politician that was being "canceled" for insisting that there were only two sexes.

"Since when is science controversial?" Jennifer posted, despite having never researched the sciences behind gender herself. She posted in support of a celebrity comic that was coming under-fire for his latest special, which was filled with anti-trans rhetoric, and a children's author that was using her platform to post gender critical essays. Jennifer saw nothing wrong with her actions.

Two days passed… and then Jennifer got sick.

It happened at a dinner party. Jennifer was wearing a tight dress and had her hair pulled away from her smooth face. She had looped her arm through Matt's and the two of them chatted idly with another doctor from Matt's department.

"You know that poor woman that made the news?" The doctor said, sniffing deeply. He had taken a snort of cocaine in the bathroom and had only done the bare minimum to hide his habit. Matt insisted that without drugs most doctors would be too exhausted to operate. Jennifer didn't really care; she only hoped that the stout doctor would offer her a bump before the night was over. It had been a whole two months since she had last ingested cocaine.

"Which woman is that?" Jennifer said.

"That trans lady that was beaten in the restroom?"

Jennifer held her tongue. She posted freely about her beliefs, but when she was surrounded by her husband and his friends, she kept her opinions locked beneath her throat.

"She's at the coma ward now." The doctor said, rubbing his nose with the heel of his hand.

"At your hospital?" Jennifer directed the question toward Matt, unsure why he hadn't told her such a thing.

Matt shrugged. "Just another patient. What's the big deal?"

"They're going to be naming a new law after her. Something about making spaces more inclusive or something. Anyways, I'm thinking of asking her sister out. She comes by to visit frequently and… what a looker!"

Jennifer ignored the doctor and looked around the room. She desperately wanted to be a part of a different conversation. One she didn't have any stake in.

Jennifer began to sift through the crowd, maneuvering away from her stocky, grey-haired husband and his portly pal. They continued to deliberate over Kellie Roth and her chances of coming up from her coma, while Jennifer took in glances from other discussions.

Dr. Morrison was talking to a pediatric nurse about crib death. Dr. Triana was engaged in a political dispute with Dr. Watts. Jennifer eventually fell alongside Dr. Mangum and his wife, who were talking about the latest Marvel movie.

"Yes, Ryan dragged me to see it and I actually enjoyed it!" Jennifer interjected with a smile.

"Oh, wasn't it just so fun?" Mangum's wife said with a smile.

Mangum grinned but said: "I prefer old horror movies… but—oh, Christ, Jenny, are you okay?"

"Hmm?" Jenny asked.

"You're… you're dribbling sweetie." The woman pointed to the corner of Jennifer's mouth.

Jennifer reached up and rubbed her lips with her hand. She inspected the limb and was shocked to see a greasy jelly trailing from her wrist to her knuckles. It reminded her of tadpole slime. A grey matter that stank of rot and infection.

"Oh." Jennifer said, mutedly.

Mangum's wife stepped toward her and took her arm. "Come along." She said. "Let's get you cleaned up. Is it puke?"

"I'm... I'm sorry. I dunno." Jennifer coughed into her palm. More jelly shot out. It was less like bile and more like cooking oil. It really stank too. It reminded her of rotten eggs and roadkill. As Jennifer and Mrs. Mangum waded through the crowd, Jennifer realized that doctors, nurses, spouses, and beneficiaries were all turning and wrinkling their noses.

What is it? Food poisoning? She had to make a note to ask her husband who their host was and which catering company they had hired. But she hadn't eaten more than a single olive with her martini! Still, *something* had done this to her.

Before she could get to the bathroom, a thread of vomit spilled out between her lips and zig-zagged across the floor in front of her. She could hear gasps of shock from all around her.

"I'm... I'm sorry." She announced in a panic. The goo was trailing down her chin and had stained the front of her dress.

"Matt?" Mrs. Mangum called.

Jennifer's husband was at her side in an instant. He led her to the bathroom and held her hair back while she vomited into the toilet. Splashing the bowl with her rancid sick, Jennifer wept with shame.

†

Of course, she spent the next day in bed; clutching her belly and throwing up in the trashcan beside her. She was shocked by the amount of fluid that roared out of her throat and into the receptacle. Halfway through the day, her son came to the door to visit her.

"Don't come in, Ryan. I've got a bug!" Jennifer said groggily, wiping her crusty mouth with a tissue. She hated being sick and she was royally embarrassed by her upchucking.

"I just wanted to check in on you." Ryan said.

"I'm fine. I'll be fine. I just... *uugh*." Jennifer leaned over her bed and made a sound like a boat engine being started. A chainsaw snarl escaped as she ejected a load of gummy, coagulated bile into the trashcan. The can was almost full to the brim. It looked like a cup containing fetid soup. Chunks of fibrous tissue and a thin membrane floated amid the syrupy expulsions.

"Gee, do you need me to bring you anything?" Ryan asked.

"Just... just... oh, God." She vomited again. The liquid pattered against the gelatinous surface of her vomit puddle. The trashcan began to overfill. Streaks of pale fluid rushed over the sides of the can and dotted the floor. "I'm... ugh..." She vomited again. Only this time, she felt a disproportionately large chunk of *something* shimmy up her throat. She began to cough and hack, forcing the mass to move up her esophagus and toward her mouth. The lumpy projectile filled her orifice, tainting her tongue with its sordid flavors.

Jennifer moaned as she wriggled her tongue against the chunky underside of the mass. It felt rocky and thick, like a hardened slab of cookie-dough. She waggled her head back and forth and coughed in an effort to get the obstacle out of her airway.

It hung out from her lips, and she realized with a spark of terror that it was as brown as tree-bark.

She hacked up the piece of fecal matter like a hairball. It dropped into the trashcan with a *plop a*nd disappeared beneath the slimy surface of her vomit.

"Mom, are you okay?" Ryan asked. He hadn't seen the piece of shit drop from her mouth, but he had witnessed her sickly grunts and groans.

"Yeah." Jennifer said stupefied by what she had just done. "I'm... I'm fine." She was lying through her teeth.

†

Jennifer made herself get out of bed.

She doused her oral cave with mouthwash and brushed her teeth over thrice. But the taste of her scat lingered on her tongue and its scent invaded her nose. She brought her puke bucket into the bathroom and dumped it into the toilet. It had fixed itself awhile back and she watched as the frothy contents of her stomach swirled down the pipe, greedily sucked up and disposed of. Now that the brackish water was clear, Jennifer felt some bands of tension loosen around her bowels and chest. It was as if she had purged something terrible from her... and now she was better.

After washing her hands and running her hair through the shower, Jennifer felt like a new woman!

It was just a bug. A terrible, horrible, awful bug. But it's gone now. You don't need to worry about it because it's gone.

Jennifer looked in the mirror. She noticed her cheeks were glowing.

But still, the taste and scent persisted.

†

Jennifer spent the rest of the day watching television. She got a call from Matt asking how she was doing, and she told him the truth:

"I'm fine. I think it's passed. Still feel a bit yucky though."

"Well, I'll be a bit late tonight coming home. Want me to bring you something?"

"No. I'm fine." Jennifer said. "I love you."

"Love you too sweetie."

He was about to hang up when Jennifer asked: "Are you taking care of... that trans... *person*?"

"Huh?" Matt asked. He didn't have a social media page, so he had no idea that his wife held such radical anti-trans sentiments.

"The one that was on the news? The one in the coma?" Jennifer said.

"Oh. No. But she's here. She's still in a coma. People keep asking about her."

"Do you... do you think she'll make it?" Jennifer hoped he'd say no. For some reason, she felt like a weight would be lifted off her chest if this woman died.

"You know how it is. No one really knows. It's just... up to her."

"Hmm." Jennifer nodded.

After saying goodbye again, Jennifer tried to focus on her show. It didn't work. Her mind kept conjuring up images of Kellie Roth, lying in her hospital bed with a hose attached to her face and her eyes swollen shut and shaded dark blue and red. She kept seeing Kellie and wondered if she was dreaming in her coma. Matt said coma patients dreamed all the time, and that some of them even remembered what they saw. She wondered if Kellie would.

Jennifer got ready for bed and went to sleep after turning the TV off.

She dreamed that she had hose shoved down her throat, and it was feeding her raw sewage.

†

Two days later, and Jennifer vomited up shit again. It happened all of a sudden while she was sitting at her favorite café. She had a psychological thriller on her lap and a coffee in her hand. When brown droplets began to rain down on the pages in front of her, she at first thought she had spilled her coffee. But then she realized what was happening.

Liquescent shit was streaming out of her mouth and soaking the pages of her book.

She sealed her lips, dropped her cup, and slapped her hands over her mouth... but she couldn't stop the fecal deluge. Her cheeks were filling, and she could feel a streamlet coursing out from her nostril and pouring down her lip and over the bumps of her fingers.

Jennifer stood like a newborn fawn on wobbly legs. She tipped back and forth before collapsing to her knees in the middle of the café. Before she could cry out, she was releasing the storm that had built up in her mouth. Musky scents filled the air as a liquid that looked like iced tea gushed out of her maw.

"Oh, God!" A barista gawked.

"Jesus!" A customer pulled her legs up so the growing puddle wouldn't touch her white sneakers.

"Someone call a doctor!" Another customer said, pointing at Jennifer as if no one else was taking note of her.

Jennifer roared as thick pebbles of solid shit crawled up her throat and plunked against the ground below her. She was leaving shit *everywhere*.

"No… no…" She said between concussive bursts. "No!"

Jennifer covered her mouth, stood, and ran away.

By the time she got to her car it was over... but her front was covered in liquid sick.

†

"What is happening to me?" Jennifer said. She had stood in the shower, fully clothed, and tried to clean up as best she could. Another wave of sickness hit her and ruined all her efforts. She then spent an hour huddled over the toilet, blasting it like it was the day after taco Tuesday... only her diarrheal stream was coming from the wrong pipe.

The old adage "better out than in" didn't apply here.

Now, the illness seemed to have stopped. But for how long?

Jennifer was scared to leave her bathroom.

"What's happening to me?" She asked and began to shudder with sorrow and anxiety. "Please, God... what's happening to *me*?"

She closed her eyes... and was struck by a vision.

Kellie Roth was lying on her hospital bed. The room around her was a blank slate. There was nothing but darkness and warmth. Kellie's face was terribly bashed.

Her lips were split, her nose was broken, and she had a tumorous lump growing beneath her brow. Her left eye was sealed shut with bruises.

Jennifer could see something in the center of Kellie's body. It was like a blue ball of fire that roared aggressively.

Jennifer was flashed back to reality. As she came back to consciousness another spewing rush of feces poured out of her mouth and decorated the mirror ahead of her. It dribbled like wet porridge into the sink, plugging the drain with blackened sea-weed-looking strips.

"It's Kellie's fault." Jennifer said as a scab of shit fell from her trembling lip and into the basin of the sink. "She's… doing this." Jennifer didn't even realize that she was no longer misgendering the woman she had mocked online only a handful of days prior.

†

After cleaning up as best she could, Jennifer went to the hospital. She came in often to visit her husband for lunch, so no one questioned her motives.

She found Kellie's room easily enough and stepped in. Indeed, the unconscious woman looked exactly as Jennifer had imagined. But the room wasn't empty. She was surrounded by flowers and cards from friends, family, and people that had been touched by her story from the news.

Jennifer looked at the cards and flowers with disgust. But her revulsion was outmatched by the growing pains in her gut. Her stomach burbled noisily, making sounds that reminded Jennifer of the dinosaurs from *Jurassic Park*.

"I want you to stop this." Jennifer moaned.

She could see the fire in Kellie's center. It burned behind her breasts and in front of her ribcage. A swirling vortex of blue light that turned a gentle pink every time Kellie's heartbeat.

"Please... it's... it's not fair." Jennifer burped. The familiar scent of rotten eggs hit her nose. "I just... I didn't beat you. I just... had an opinion—"

Jennifer felt as if she had been punched in the gut. She doubled over and a stream of stool splashed against the floor. To her shock, she could see that the icky liquid was laced with blood. Thick wads of tissue clung to the shitty surface of her newfound puddle.

Oh, God! Jennifer pleaded internally. She looked up, begging for mercy. But Kellie was still.

"Please!" Jennifer honked. "I just had an opinion!" Another roiling storm blew through her. This time, she could *feel* something detach inside her and begin its slow trek up her throat. "We just don't see eye-to-eye, Kellie! Please, you don't have to... kill me!"

Blood began to seep between Jennifer's teeth. It was as if being near Kellie was accelerating her digestive destruction.

Another vision hit Jennifer.

Ryan had gone into the bathroom after Jennifer had finished. Wearing yellow kitchen gloves, he lifted the lid and gingerly scooped out a pebble of his mother's feces. He looked disgusted but resolved.

While Jennifer sat on her phone, Ryan took her excrement into his room.

Ryan put a sewing needle through it and wrapped the speared pebble in red twine. Delicately, he held the fetish next to his heart and began to chant. It was a low murmur. Jennifer couldn't decipher the words, but she knew he wasn't praying to God.

At least, not the God she worshiped.

He set the item on the floor and kissed it. No hesitation. No revulsion. He kissed her poo before lighting three wax candles and stripping off his clothes.

To her shock, Jennifer had to watch as he masturbated.

Upon completion... a shadowy form grew in the corner of his room. Jennifer watched as the figure stepped forward and reached down for the waxy puddle of semen that had been dashed against her impaled scat.

The demon picked up the item... and swallowed it.

The vision faded away... and Jennifer was hurled into the dark. She could see her son, and he had a blue light in his chest. It was identical to Kellie's. Then, she saw another figure.

A teenaged girl with curly hair and misty eyes.

"I... I wish I didn't have to be your secret, Ryan." She said as she kissed Jennifer's son.

"Me too, Lucy." Ryan said.

They were sitting in the park, far away from prying eyes. The teenaged girl had a fire roaring in her chest. The same shade of blue.

"But you know my mom. She's..."

"A bigot?" Lucy said.

"She doesn't think she is. She thinks she's a feminist. You know what she calls herself? A TERF. A trans exclusive radical feminist!"

"I've heard the term, Mr. Exposition." Lucy rolled her beautiful green eyes.

"I just... I just don't want her to know about you. Because then she'll hate you. And I don't want a single person on this planet to hate you."

Ryan kissed Lucy.

And Jennifer realized that he had cast this spell to prevent his own mother from knowing that he was in love. That she had driven him to this. That she... deserved this.

Jennifer was flung away from the vision of her son and his girlfriend, and found she was alone in an empty room with a mirror.

She could see her naked form... and the fire in her chest. Unlike Kellie, Lucy, and Ryan... Jennifer's fire was grey and curled. Her hatred had turned it into a chunk of diseased scat.

Jennifer was thrust back into her body. She landed on her hands and knees and heaved. A purple tube snaked out of her mouth and splashed against the vomit-strewn floor. Jennifer pinched her eyes shut... and helplessly listened as her guts and innards began to spool out from their inner chambers. Her stomach seemed to deflate, and her throat was rubbed raw as vital organs slopped out of her mouth. Her teeth scratched organs apart and her mouth was drenched in acids, enzymes, and bloody rags of tissue.

Oh, God... please... let me die. Jennifer thought.

God wouldn't accept Jennifer into His heaven... but a dark figure that appeared in the corner welcomed her with clawed hands and serrated teeth.

SOMETHING AKIN TO REVULSION

REHEARSAL

The very idea of holding a party on a Sunday —a school night—was a disaster in the making. And so, Corky wasn't all that surprised that things had gone dreadfully wrong by the time it got dark out. For one, no one had thought to bring any booze. It was like a junior high shindig all over again, with mopey teens standing like wallflowers or lost in sloppy kissing pools. Conversation was banal at best, frustrating at worse. When everyone was sober, nobody had anything fun to say.

And Corky was pretty sure that the same song had played three times on Lindsey's playlist.

But it wasn't Corky's party... so it wasn't her disaster. She was simply a witness, forced to watch as a heinous crime wasted their Sunday afternoon.

"This *sucks*." Rand said and scratched the back of his head. His fingers got tangled in his curly hair and he began to pick at the knots.

Rand was Corky's best friend. Both had an unyielding interest in video games and true-crime podcasts. Now that they were out of their school uniforms, Corky was wearing a t-shirt with John Wayne Gacy's mugshot on it. Rand was wearing a shirt with an image of a jumping 8-bit Mario.

Corky was a pretty girl, with a sharp nose and short hair dyed purple. Their school –a strict private academy—had raised hell about her hair but there was nothing that could be done about it until the dye wore itself out. And they weren't going to expel their reigning mathlete over a superfluous fashion statement.

Rand wore glasses and had started to grow a beard. It looked like a wispy tuft of goat-fur, but he was obnoxiously proud of it and made a great show out of stroking it. Were Corky excelled in math, Rand was a total computer geek. He spent his free time in the family basement –dubbed 'The Dungeon'—working of programs that Corky could barely understand or comprehend. He insisted that he wanted to be an app developer, but he spent more time hacking local news stations and adjusting their teleprompter to say something ludicrous.

Corky Shaw loved Rand Norton. He was like a younger brother to her, even though they were both juniors. And so, when Corky was invited to Lindsey Rake's Sunday night party, she hadn't hesitated to invite Rand. Now, she wished neither of them had come over.

"We could be doing… literally anything else." Rand said and sipped at an aluminum can of off-brand soda. He shuddered and set the can down on Lindsey's coffee-table. He didn't bother to move a coaster over. Leaving a ring on the oak surface of her coffee-table seemed as close to a middle-finger as they'd be able to throw.

"The night's still young." Corky sighed and looked toward the wall-clock. *It really wasn't*. At almost eight, she'd need to go home if she wanted to get a few hours of rest in before school. Not that this Monday would be an important one. There were no tests, no homework assignments due, and the mathletes didn't have practice until Wednesday night.

But still, she didn't want to walk in with dark bags under her brown eyes.

"Let's call it a night, okay?" Rand offered with a grey smile. "This party is—" He suddenly tilted his frown into a smile and adjusted his tone. "—*awesome*! Hey, Linds!"

Lindsey plopped onto the sofa between Rand and Corky. She draped her arms over both of them and giggled serenely. Lindsey was small, blonde-haired, and her face was heart shaped. She reminded Corky of an over-eager kindergartener that had a million stories to tell but wanted to tell them all at once.

"Isn't this great?" Lindsey asked and swept her eyes from side to side. "I just can't believe how many people showed!"

Corky looked around the room. There were probably only ten people here with them, and none of them swam in the same circles. There was a kid with a horror movie t-shirt struggling to make conversation with a guy wearing a Cardinal's cap. The only thing either of them shared was discomfort.

"Yeah. Real good turnout." Rand threw his head back and stared up at the ceiling. Was he trying to hide a grimace?

Corky smiled and patted Lindsey's shoulder. "Well, I may have to turn in soon."

"Oh, c'mon!" Lindsey squealed. "I've got a surprise guest coming!"

What a weird thing to say, Corky thought as Lindsey grunted her way up to her feet and went around accosting her other guests with hugs.

"A surprise guest? Who is it? Frank Grillo? Steven Seagal? I hear they're desperate for work." Rand quipped. "What about Shawn William Scott? Has he been doing anything lately?"

"I think he's on TV. Or he's doing indie films." Corky shrugged. "Who could she be talking about?"

"I don't even know." Rand said and picked up his off-brand soda and took another sip. "God this shit tastes weird."

"Yeah, I wish she had some beer or something." Corky sighed and rubbed her eyes with the heels of her palms.

"Wanna go check the garage? Maybe her dad had some stored away."

"No." Corky said. "I really just want to go home and get some sleep."

"I think we should stay just to see who the surprise guest is." Rand laughed. "I mean, what if it's Mel Gibson?"

"I definitely *don't* want to hang out with Mel Gibson."

"Oh, c'mon. You know he'll say some interesting things." Rand chided.

"Racist things." Corky stretched like a cat. "Besides, I don't think Lindsey could afford a celebrity guest star. It's probably her older cousin with some beer... or her weed dealer. I honestly don't care."

"Can we joke about celebrities anyways?" Rand scratched at his beard. "You know, I hope I never get famous. Famous people always end up miserable."

"You spend your days in the Dungeon hacking into porn sites for fun. You really don't need to worry about the high-life." Corky scowled.

"Hey, I don't hack porn sites. My feminism *includes* sex workers." Rand said. If he had made that joke to anyone else, they may have been offended. But Corky just laughed.

Suddenly, the kid in the horror tee shirt collapsed. He dropped to the ground as if a hammer had struck the back of his head.

Corky gasped and leapt to her feet, covering her mouth with both hands.

"Oh, my god!" The kid with the baseball cap dropped his soda. It began to bubble out of its top and spread a hissing puddle across the ground.

"Somebody, call an ambulance!" Corky yelled as Rand jumped over the coffee-table and knelt by the convulsing kid.

"Is he having a seizure?" A girl with pigtails asked.

"I don't know." Rand admitted and helped the boy turn over so that he was facing the floor. "But I don't want him to choke if he starts ralphing."

It was good thinking, Corky realized, even if Rand's words were ineloquent.

A girl took out her phone and began to dial 9-11. But then, she fell over too. Her head struck the corner of the coffee-table and a spurt of blood splashed across its oak surface. She began to rattle against the floor, wheezing for breath as her injury took her life.

Corky screamed again and watched as –one by one—the entire party began to fall down onto the ground. They dropped onto their knees and pitched forward, smacking the ground aggressively. Some shook in place, while others lay totally still.

Something was wrong. Something was terribly wrong.

Corky looked around for help but realized that even Rand had fallen victim to the strange phenomenon.

And then, Corky saw Lindsey opening the garage door and letting her surprise guest walk in.

He was tall and handsome, and Corky recognized him instantly. Her shock overwhelmed her, and her mouth went dry.

"Oh, my God. It's… it's… *you*."

"Didn't she drink the soda?" The man said.

"I thought she had." Lindsey shrugged. Her chipper vibe had become diluted. Her eyes gleamed, but their intent was sinister.

"Oh well. Gonna have to do this the hard way then." The young man lurched toward Corky. Before she could even think to run, he had her in his arms and he was suppressing her with a chokehold. Corky battered his arms with her fists and tried to claw his face, but he moved around like a thrashing alligator. In a matter of moments, Corky felt her vision blur and her body alight with tingles.

No. Corky thought. *No, God. Please, God. No. No. No.*

The man drew her toward the ground. Before he laid her down, she was knocked cold.

†

Corky awoke with a start. She jerked at her hands and found them restrained to the armrests of a folding chair. She had been strapped down with duct-tape, and her mouth was sealed with a rubbery ball-gag.

She wasn't the only one in the room. Across from her sat Rand, and next to him was a girl she recognized from the hallways at school but didn't know. She was Asian and her hair was tied up in a knot. Her eyes were filled with tears and her cheeks throbbed behind a similar gag. All three of them were tied down.

In the corner lay a pile of bodies. The other guests had all died. Poisoned by whatever foul ingredient had been added to the soda.

"It's really a shame." Lindsey said, kicking at the dented head of the girl that had hit the coffee-table. A strand of mucus-y brain goop leaked out of the fissure in her hairline. "I wanted a few more to make it. Just so we could really get it down, you know? I wanted more practice."

"Three's good enough." A new voice said. Scratchy and weird. She knew it too. He was a classmate. She turned and found Stew Whitley standing by the side of her chair. His red hair was slicked with sweat, and his double chin was bursting with acne. Stew was in mathletes. Corky knew him. Not incredibly well, but enough to chat with him when he was bagging her mother's groceries at the *Shop & Save*.

"Three's good. One for each of us." He said with a leering grin. "Hey, Corky! You're up! *Good*. Now we can get this shit-show started!"

Corky's assailant came out of the hall bathroom. He had put a band-aide over his left brow. Apparently, one of Corky's scratches had found its mark.

Kip Riedell was someone Corky had never thought she'd see again. He had been expelled from school in his senior year after a rumor had been proven true. Kip was accused of assaulting a girl in the locker room after volleyball practice. He had hidden inside a locker and waited for one of the girls to be there by herself, and he had attacked her. Like a savage predator. He had also shoved her head into the locker and closed the door on it. He had left her with two black eyes, a split mouth, multiple broken teeth, and a pregnant belly. Corky hadn't seen her crammed into her locker post-rape, but a few of her teammates had. One had even been cruel enough to take a photo, and it had traveled infamously around the school. Corky was thankful the degrading photo had never crawled into any of her inboxes, and if it had she was certain she wouldn't have looked at it.

Corky couldn't remember the girl's name. They hadn't been friends. But she knew that she had moved out of town, even after Kip had been expelled.

Of course, in true American judicial fashion, Kip had turned on the waterworks and the judge gave him a short sentence... so as not to affect his future *too* gravely. Corky remembered the controversy, the angry Facebook posts, and the photos on the news of Kip joyously walking out of the courthouse in handcuffs. She also remembered his lawyer insisting that the "justice system proved its worth by treating a young man with a bright future with fairness and mercy". She had also heard Kip's own father say in a news interview: "don't let one mistake ruin my son's life." That phrase had filled Corky with indignation and rage.

And now... now he was here.

Jesus. He's already out of jail? It only happened last year. Corky thought.

Kip grinned toward Lindsey. He took her by the waist and pulled her in for a kiss. Their lips locked together and their hands crawling up each other's bodies... they both looked starved.

Were they dating before it happened? Did she know he had planned to rape that poor girl? Was she… involved? Corky thought.

After separating, Kip addressed the room.

"My friends and I have big plans for tomorrow. And in order to execute our plans to perfection, we'd all like… a little practice." Kip pulled at his pants and coughed. "Because as we all know, practice makes perfect."

The three victims shouted behind their ball gags. Rand kicked his head back and forth. He was tied down so tightly his fingers had turned blue.

The female student began to piss herself. A clear current drained out of the bottoms of her jeans and pooled between her ankles. Corky wished she could get the poor girl a towel, but her legs had gone to sleep beneath her duct-tape bondage.

The corpses in the corner were already beginning to smell. Several of them had voided their bowels and the blood rising from the girl's damaged head was as sharp as spice.

Corky screeched beneath her gag. She wanted it out of her mouth. She could feel bile racing up her throat and filling her oral cavity as the reality of the situation hit her.

She was going to die… and there was *nothing* she could do to stop it.

Corky began to cough, choking on the rancid puke that clogged her mouth and throat. A vile stream of belly-slime began to leak out of the space between the rubber ball and her lips. It drained down her chin and spattered against her chest. She made a noise like a boat motor being yanked and rolled her eyes into her skull.

The clasp behind her head was undone and the gag was jerked away from her orifice. A stream of upchuck sailed out of her and splattered against the ground.

Tired –and a bit embarrassed— Corky struggled to get her breath back. She looked up and saw that Stew was grinning down at her. He held up the oily, gleaming gag and said:

"I found these in my Momma's closet. I can only wonder where they've been."

Corky closed her eyes and began to sob. "Please. Just let us go. Please."

Stew grabbed a handful of her short hair and pulled her upright so that she was facing Rand.

"You little bitch. All that flirting at the grocery store, and you never *once* gave me the time of day at school." Stew whispered.

"I wasn't… I was just *talking* to you, you sick fuck!" Her anger was back.

"Let her go, Stew." Kip pointed to the cut on his brow. "That one's mine."

Stew growled like a distempered dog. That lasted until Kip pointed to the other girl. "But you can have Becky."

Stew stepped away from Corky and dropped her gag.

Corky could see the terror in Becky's eyes. None of them knew what Kip was talking about, but it couldn't be good. Not knowing made it worse. Way worse.

Rand began to shout something, but it was muffled. Still, Corky could understand a significant piece of it. Rand said: "Take me! Not them!" It was a noble but fruitless offer.

Stew crossed the room. He lumbered like a bear, sucking in angry breaths through his crooked teeth. Corky had never realized just how ugly he was until now. His face was blistered, his lips were chapped, and his teeth were piss yellow. But then again, she had never known that his true personality was so monstrous either. All she really knew about him was that he was great at fractions and liked to play *Call of Duty* when he wasn't at school or work.

"Let's watch." Lindsey said into Kip's ear. Corky saw her hand crawl between Kip's legs and squeeze his junk. Kip's eyes fluttered and he released a long exhalation.

Stew walked by Becky and stooped down behind the sofa. He came back up, holding a black duffle bag, which he set on the coffee-table. Delicately —as if he was undressing a lover— he unzipped the bag.

Becky began to scream anew when Stew reached in and pulled out a screwdriver.

Rand began to rock back and forth in his seat, arguing in ineligible spurts. The ball-gag had muted him totally, and Corky wished he wouldn't waste his effort.

Stew walked up and took Becky by the throat. She gagged and her nose began to leak a green porridge. Stew leaned in close and swept the mucus up with his tongue. He prodded her nostrils with his pink tongue, as if he was probing a tasty dessert. He pulled his head back and smacked his lips. He looked toward Lindsey and Kip with a smile.

"Tastes salty!" He declared.

"You're fucking sick, dude." Kip laughed as he undid his pants and let Lindsey reach into their dank recesses. She began to stroke him under his clothes, moaning as if she was the one being pleasured.

Stew stood and held the screwdriver beneath Becky's chin. He poked her quickly. She reeled back, yelping with fright the second the cool metal touched her.

Stew began to shush her and stroke her hair. "Hey, Becky… it'll be okay. Hold still. Just hold still."

Stew drew the screwdriver along the line of her jaw. He stopped at her chin and rotated the sharp end of the tool at its center. He was *teasing* her, the demented maniac.

You don't want to see this. A reasonable voice said in Corky's head. But she didn't obey it. She couldn't look away.

Even as Stew brought the screwdriver up and began to invade Becky's left nostril with it.

If Becky had been screaming before, she began to wail now.

More snot gushed out of the hole, followed by a thick and sludgy mudslide of blood and loosened tissue. Before even a second had passed, Stew had the screwdriver up to its hilt. Its head was buried in her.

Becky began to convulse in her seat. Her hands opened and closed against the armrests. They tightened up and turned white. Almost impossibly, her right eye curled up and turned blind. Her left eye bugged out of its socket.

With a grunt, Stew pulled the tool free. It was followed by a cascade of blood.

Corky had seen her fair share of horror movies. In those, the blood seemed to ebb out of the victim. But that wasn't how it worked in real life. The blood *fell* out of Becky's molested nose. Like wine from a broken bottle.

"God! That feels so good." Stew said and stepped back, admiring the leakage he had caused. "Do ya'all *see* that?"

"Ain't looking at nothing else." Kip laughed and pulled Lindsey's hand out of his drawers. It was glistening with pre-ejaculate. "Now, make sure she's dead."

"Right." Stew nodded. He took Becky's face and turned it upwards. Blood shot out and greased his fingers. He pushed the screwdriver up her other nostril with an audible *crunch*. He jammed it in as high as it would go… before he began to stir.

Corky finally looked away, certain that she was going to vomit again.

"You're turn, babes." Kip said and patted Lindsey's rear. "Hop to it."

Lindsey strolled to the bag and took her time picking a weapon. It was clear that Rand was her target. He began to screech for mercy again, but still he went unheard. Even if he wasn't impeded by the gag, Corky was sure that the deviant killers wouldn't have listened.

They were crazy. That was the only explanation Corky had. Kip, Stew, and Lindsey were all absolutely fucking nuts. Like a band of merry degenerates from an exploitation film… they were *delighted* by the torment that they were causing.

"Sick." Corky said as saliva poured out of her mouth. The tangy taste of vomit still clung to her tongue.

Kip whirled around and snarled. "I'll tell you what's sick… expecting me to just *go away* after you all ruined my life." He patted Rand's shoulder before gripping it tightly. "This isn't sick. This… *this is justice*."

So not only was he disturbed… he was delusional too.

Lindsey stood up. She had found her implement of choice. Rand's eyes grew wide when he realized that Lindsey was carrying a circular pizza cutter. She flicked her finger against its smooth side, spinning the blade with a light hiss.

"Get his pants open." Lindsey said.

"No! Stop!" Corky pleaded in defense of her best friend. "Please! We didn't do anything to you!"

"You did. You totally did." Kip said as he pulled Rand's belt away and undid his trousers. Rand's eyes rolled back, and he briefly fainted before Kip roused him awake by yanking his penis out from his checkered boxers. "You *all* deserve this."

Lindsey reached down and plucked at Rand's limp cock.

"How? What did we do? Please… can't you just stop?" Corky bellowed.

Lindsey held Rand's tube upright and pressed the blade against his piss-slit. Urine began to spray out of his penis. It slid up the sides of the blade and splashed Lindsey's face. She laughed and began to drag the pizza cutter down the length of his cock. Corky watched as the flesh unzipped and revealed the veins and muscles beneath. A soft stuffing began to ooze out, like melted marshmallow cream. It was followed by a red stream.

Rand screamed even harder now. The pain must have been unbearable.

Corky wept as her best friend was mutilated.

Lindsey set the pizza cutter down and began to work the skin away from Rand's penis. Totally de-gloved, it looked like a red strand of meat. An uncooked pipe of sausage. A veiny branch, drizzled with strawberry syrup.

Lindsey put her head between Rand's thighs and began to suckle the mutilated organ. Instead of pleasure, she caused pain. Rand jolted and sweated and yelped as Lindsey used her teeth to shave away layers of vital tissue from his bleeding hose.

Stew stepped aside. "Whoa. I feel overshadowed." He laughed. "Lindsey, you are *so* totally fucked."

Lindsey then bit down. Rand shouted. Corky wailed. Stew and Kip exclaimed in delight and watched as Lindsey pulled her head away from Rand's groin, dragging his manhood out from his pelvic cavity. It popped loose with a noise that reminded Corky of paper being torn. Then, there followed the sound of wet plopping. She saw that Rand's body was jettisoning his blood through the hole where his penis had once sat. It sprayed Lindsey like a scarlet money-shot.

She chewed the penis-meat sloppily, allowing chunks to trickle out of her stuffed mouth and dribble onto the floor. She licked her fingers and crooned with delight.

"Fucking brutal!" Stew shouted and applauded.

Corky hadn't thought Lindsey was capable of any form of violence until this moment. She hadn't known the girl all that well –obviously—but she had always seemed so sweet and mild-mannered. She was a Christian, for crying out loud! She was part of the group of geeks that stood around the flagpole and prayed every morning! Corky had never thought she'd be capable of eating a man's junk… much less enjoying it!

Corky looked toward Rand. His face had gone pale, and his eyes were flickering in and out of consciousness. The pain was more than he was capable of bearing.

"I'm sorry." Corky said, as if any of this was her fault.

Lindsey stood, holding the pizza cutter aloft. Without ceremony, she cut open Rand's throat. The searing wound spurted blood across her already stained front. Lindsey sighed and tilted her head back, allowing the warm fluids to decorate her.

After a moment, her show was over, and Rand was lifeless. "What are you going to do to her, baby?" Lindsey lifted her head. It was smeared in red body-sauce.

Kip shucked his shoulders and reached behind his back. "I don't want to spoil my appetite. I'll do something… incredible tomorrow. This was all just a rehearsal. When we go to school tomorrow… we'll make *this* look like a goddamn picnic!"

"Please! Let me go!" Corky wailed.

Kip pulled out a handgun from behind his trousers.

"I wish you could see what all we're going to do. We have so many people on our list, it isn't even funny. And we're going to get too them too, hon. One by one." Corky couldn't tell if Kip was talking to his friends, or to her.

Kip strolled over to her and began to fit the gun into her opened mouth. She tried to close her lips, but the shirked upward after touching the polished surface of the weapon. She felt her teeth clack against it as Kip rotated the gun so that its snout was pressed against the roof of her mouth. He looked over and beamed at his blood-soaked friends. Lindsey and Stew were all-smiles.

Corky inhaled.

It was the last sound she made before a bullet plowed through her brain and tore it out the top of her head. The last thought she had was this:

Maybe I'm one of the lucky ones--

SOMETHING AKIN TO REVULSION

BODY-CRUNCH

Elmo Pabst had been wrestling for Titus for three years now. It was an easy gig for someone like Elmo. Elmo was big and tough... and he had a record. The kind of record that made regular employers flinch and cringe. The sort of record that made finding constant and consistent work a challenge. The kind of record that required him to knock on doors and introduce himself to new neighbors with a warning. But no one cared about *all that* in the Ring.

The Ring was set up behind Titus's barn on his forty-acre farm. It comprised of a wooden platform topped with cushioned pads. The pads did little to soften a real fall or blow, but this was a dirty game for dirty players. None of that pussy-shit made it far with *this* audience.

There were four wooden posts lashed together with bungee cords. The Ring was nothing special. In fact, it looked as if it had been constructed by children. But once a week, a group of yokels and rednecks would gather around and bet on fights. They didn't need fancy costumes, cool backstories, or dazzling shows to be entertained. They just wanted to watch two dudes —and maybe two chicks on a rare occasion—duke it out until someone was unconscious.

Elmo was Titus Candy's prize stud.

Elmo's checkered past had been like a beacon for Titus. The older man apparently made a habit of picking up the local scuzz-buckets and making something of them. When Elmo wasn't fighting in the Ring, he was peddling drugs to high schoolers. Either way, he was getting paid in cash by Titus on a weekly basis.

Elmo at first thought that working for Titus would be depressing, but he had come to feel strangely affirmed by his newfound position in life. For one, Elmo was handsomer than Titus and his cronies. When they went out, Elmo was the catch of the group. Elmo was tall and lean, with a bald head and a crooked nose, and he wore a goatee.

"You look like a Satanist." Titus had once laughed. "Especially when you wear sunglasses. You look like you cut up babies and goats every night!"

Of course, Titus never directly referenced Elmo's crimes, and he was quick to shut the topic down when it was brought up. According to Titus, everyone deserved a second chance. Even pedophiles.

It was almost midnight and Elmo had one last fight left. Titus stood by his prize-fighter's side and spoke in a low voice.

"Don't worry. This one will be a piece of cake." Titus grinned devilishly. "The guy is simple. Managed by his brother. A real George and Lenny pair, you know?"

Elmo had never read *Of Mice and Men*, but he nodded anyways and scrubbed his teeth with a finger. One of them was loose but his mind was too fogged with coke to tell which one. He had just fought Greg Haberdasher and Frankie Lewis. Frankie was a dwarf, but he was like a human cannonball. He had driven his small head into Elmo's guts with so much force Elmo had thought he was going to cough up his spleen. One more fight seemed like too much, but each fight was another handful of cash and Elmo *needed* the money. Rent was due.

Titus was rotund and grey-haired. His eyes were droopy, and his teeth were stained with nicotine scars. He held a moist cigar between his fish-lips, and he compulsively tugged at his crotch with a hairy hand.

"It's the kid's first fight. I told them to throw it. Just... make sure it looks like he's getting the best of you before you swing him down. Okay?"

"Yeah. Sure." Elmo said and sat down on the nearest lawn chair. He looked around at the last remnants of the crowd. Most of the spectators had gone home, and a good forty percent of them had been too drunk to pay attention to a fight anyways. The last audience members were younger folks. There was a twenty-year-old with horn-rimmed glasses and a backwards baseball cap. There was a group of kids who looked about fifteen. They must have snuck away from home to catch the fights. *Wasn't it a school night*? Elmo sneered and lurched forward, tucking his head into his palms.

"Hey? Are you doing, okay?" Titus asked. "You ain't gonna hurl, are you?"

"Nah. I'm fine. Just ready for bed. Am I bleeding? From the gums?" Elmo threw Titus a smile.

"You're good. Here, hit this rock. On the house." Titus passed Elmo a hazy pipe.

"This kid strong?"

"No. Well. He's big. He's actually kind of a fatty." Titus laughed, as if he had a perfect waistline.

Elmo blinked, and then he was back on the padded "Ring". He swayed on his ankles, letting his hands fall loose by his sides. They didn't wear boxing gloves, kneepads, or mouthguards in Titus's Ring. The good folks of Kirkland, Missouri, paid to see authentic punches. Even if the winners were decided beforehand... each blow was *real*.

The Ring was illuminated by the floodlights perched atop Titus Candy's pickup. It was barely enough for Elmo to see in front of him. He'd basically be fighting blind.

But then, as if God was listening to Elmo's critiques, a bolt of lightning scratched at the clouds above them. In its brief appearance, Elmo's opponent was visible.

Elmo realized that Titus had dramatically undersold the newbie.

Elmo's opponent was obese, indeed. But he was no run-of-the-mill "fatty". The man, clambering between the bungee cords and worming his way into the Ring, was at least five hundred and fifty pounds. Maybe he was six hundred. It was hard to tell.

His every movement caused a ripple. The very structure of the Ring seemed to bend beneath him. The man's face was grizzled with acne scars and fresh pimples, clustered together. He was so pock-marked; his face looked like an oozing honeycomb. Elmo could see white calk clumped around the rolled corners of his mouth.

The lightning was gone, and so too was Elmo's view. Instead, the man became a dense and overwhelming shadow. A massive cloak that steadied itself at the opposite end of the Ring.

Another crack of lighting bloomed across the sky, and Elmo was treated to further horrors. He could see now that the man was shirtless, but his sweatpants were creased with sweat crust. And it was obvious he wasn't wearing underwear. A wiry thatch of pubic hair grew over the rim of his sweats, clumped between his belly rolls like wet moss amidst a bevy of heavy boulders. His pubes seemed to be the only body hair that had filled in. His face was baby-smooth, and his head was totally bald. Even his *head* was filled with fat. The rumples looked like fleshy cornrows.

Elmo continued to stare, looking the mammoth up and down. When his eyes connected to his opponent's, the monster-man smiled childishly, exposing a row of nasty, unwashed teeth.

Elmo looked outside of the Ring for Titus. Instead, he saw a fiendishly twiggy individual standing close by. His eyes were trained on the behemoth. Elmo recognized his expression: *pride*. The skinny man was the large man's brother. His "manager".

Elmo sighed, puffed up his chest, and tore his shirt off in one fluid motion. His arms were lassoed with muscle and his chest was berated with bruises. He flexed and posed, showing off for the miniscule crowd. He hoped he was also intimidating the large beast on the opposite side of the Ring. But he doubted it.

He could use you as a toothpick.

Elmo grunted and crossed his arms together. He tried to look tough, but he knew that his eyes were betraying him. He knew... he was scared.

Titus crawled up onto the Ring and stood at its center. He held up his hands, as if he was shushing the already still and silent crowd. He spoke up in a raspy boom:

"You all know him; you all love him… our very own Elmo 'The Rumble' Pabst!" There was a round of scattered and weak applause. "Let's give it up for 'The Rumble'!" Titus commanded and the applause grew louder. Someone even built up the gumption to whistle —God bless them. "You've seen him bleed… and you've seen him *make motherfuckers bleed*!"

Elmo flexed his arms again and this time the cheers were genuine.

"But… Elmo may have met his match! Blown in straight from the deep, deep, *DEEP* heart of Texas, we're proud to introduce to the Ring… the formidable… the massive… *Freak*."

It was a fitting moniker. Elmo couldn't deny it.

The applause tapered off. The Freak didn't seem to care about the crowd. He was looking up toward the heavens in slack-jawed wonder.

"Let's get ready to--!"

The Freak suddenly careened forward. He almost collided with Titus, but the older man was able to sidestep the monstrosity. Titus skittered away from the Ring on hot feet, as if he had dodged a train. Elmo wasn't so lucky. He was standing directly in the Freak's path. He was too stunned to even throw a punch. He just let the Freak plow into him, throwing him toward the Ring's edge. His back connected to a wooden post and Elmo let out a harsh wheeze before the Freak threw a fist into his lower jaw. Elmo felt his teeth snap together.

"Jesus!" Someone in the audience screamed.

The Freak threw another punch. This one slammed into Elmo's temple. He was blinded, disoriented, and unable to steady himself. He fell forward and into the Freak's slimy chest.

The Freak's skin was oily, sweaty, and smelled like mold. Elmo tried to squirm away from the blanket of fatty skin, but already the Freak was holding him in a bear hug. Squeezing him.

He's gotta let go. Elmo thought. *I'll die if I have to keep smelling him.*

Elmo drove a fist into the Freak's belly. The fat acted as both cushioning and armor. He doubted the big man had even felt it.

From the corner of the Ring, the Freak's nimble brother shouted out: "Get him, Oren!"

Knowing the Freak's name was good. Maybe he could reason with him. Elmo choked out a quick sentence: "Please, lemme go. Oren. You've gotta let me go."

The Freak looked down at Elmo, bemusement and humor crossing over his rumpled face. The sort of look a dog gave its master when its name was called. Elmo smiled and wormed around between the Freak's massive limbs.

The Freak squeezed him even closer. The sudden crushing power of the Freak's arms forced Elmo to inhale. The suction drew in some of the Freak's moldy flesh. Elmo felt as if he was swallowing a fist. He coughed and hacked dramatically.

This is all part of the show. Titus said they agreed to throw the match. I just gotta make a convincing struggle. Elmo thought. *Well, there's no faking this! This dude could kill me!*

Elmo did the only thing he could think of. He bit down. His teeth sank into the meat between the Freak's massive breasts. He felt blood and gristle well up around his lips. A repulsive stink oozed into his nasal cavity.

The Freak reacted strongly.

He pushed Elmo away.

Elmo tipped over and landed on his back. Winded, sputtering, and weary, he lay at the Ring's floor. He looked up into the night sky and at the dancing streams of lightning which illuminated their backwoods fight.

He heard the Freak stamp around in a mean circle, clutching at his wounded chest and shouting like a distempered child. The Freak seemed incapable of forming a coherent sentence, but his wet voice managed a few choice words:

"Fucker! Fucker! Ouchy! Fucker!"

From Elmo's corner, Titus shouted out to the crowd: "I promised you blood, didn't I?"

The fool thought that this was Elmo's win. It wasn't. It was nearly a desperate bid for an extended life. The Freak didn't comprehend that this was even a game. Elmo knew this already. Elmo knew he was *fighting for his life.*

The Freak's brother knew it too because he shouted: "Oren! Let it go, buddy! Calm down!"

But it was too late. The Freak ran up to Elmo's crippled body and stomped down between his legs.

Elmo's crotch seemed to deflate beneath the elephantine foot. He could hear a *crack* resound through his body as his pelvic bone snapped like a twig. And then, his balls were trapped between the Freak's heel and the wooden platform. They popped apart, spewing testicle mucus and blood down Elmo's thighs.

Elmo sat upright and cried out. His shout was canceled by the Freak's meaty fist, which collided with his mouth and sent his head snapping backwards. Laid flat, his testicles and his pelvis smashed, and his mouth filling with blood… Elmo felt defeated.

Good. It's over. Titus will take me to the hospital. I'm done. I'm tapped out.

But it wasn't over. The Freak wasn't done with Elmo.

He crouched over Elmo's twitching body and smiled down at him, his whole head obscuring Elmo's view of the night sky. Drool hung in thick strands down the Freak's rolling chins. His beady eyes seemed to bloom like flowers between his sloping brow and crusty cheeks. He looked serene and happy.

With a whoosh of hot air, the Freak lifted his legs and dropped his entire body weight onto Elmo's stomach.

Butt first.

The collision was like dropping a cinderblock onto a tube of toothpaste.

Elmo felt something *slimy* explode out of his backside, followed by a wormy rope of intestines. Simultaneously, his last meal —a roasted turkey sandwich—ejaculated out of his throat. Streams of acidic vomit sprayed out of his nostrils as well.

The Freak rolled away and crawled up to his feet. He victoriously raised his arms above his head, expecting a round of applause. All he was met with were screams.

"Oh, Jesus!" The Freak's brother shouted. "Oren! What did you *do*?"

Elmo turned over and reached between his legs. His pants were filled with more than just feces. He could feel a foot's worth of internal piping coiled up in his underwear. The Freak had forced his guts out of his anus with one blow.

Elmo wheezed and felt a massive amount of pressure move from his guts to his rear. Even more of his belly-contents were pouring out of him. A musky, brown river streamed down his thighs. The liquid felt hot and snotty.

Elmo coughed and seized his aching belly. Tears grew out of his sore eyes. He began to mewl like a starved puppy. His whole body was rocked with pain.

"Oh, dear God!" Titus slinked onto the stage. "Oh, dear God!"

"Titus…" Elmo groaned. "Titus… I don't feel too good."

"Oh, Christ." Titus knelt down by Elmo and cupped his head into his hands. He gagged and shuddered, turning his face away from Elmo. Elmo couldn't blame him. Elmo could smell the mushed contents in his drawers. It was like a pound of damp roadkill. The combination of internal stew with blood was like a wall of pungency.

He could hear the audience stampeding away. He could hear the thin brother attempting to drag Oren off stage. He could hear the thunder and lightning above him.

Elmo heard the pattering of rain across the platform. It was finally coming down.

SOMETHING AKIN TO REVULSION

COKE-NAIL

"She has a coke-nail. You ever notice that?" Rod asked.

"Huh?" I looked up from my phone. We had been smoking in Rod's basement, and Rod had put *The Empire Strikes Back* on. Rod was into that type of shit. I never really cared for *Star Wars*. Or movies in general.

"What are you talking about?" Gerri asked with a slushy cough. She was getting over covid, and we were all sitting a few feet away from her, even though she had assured us she was no longer contagious.

"Carrie Fisher. Look at her pinky nail. It's longer than any of her others. People would grow out a nail so they could scoop coke up on it back in the day."

"I love Carrie Fisher." Gerri said.

"Oh, shit. You're right." I said, squinting at the TV. Princess Leia's hand was resting on Han's shoulder, and we could all see her elongated fingernail. I'd watched *Star Wars* before, of course, but I had never realized that. Not that I had ever really paid too much attention to that show. It was a bunch of nerd shit and I hate nerd shit. I've never played a videogame before, I don't collect comic books, and I'd rather suffocate on a sandwich bag than watch a Marvel movie on opening night. It was honestly weird that I considered Rod and Gerri my best pals, because they ate that garbage up with a spoon. Even now, Rod's shirt featured a character from *My Hero Academia* and Gerri had an *Autobot* icon tattooed on her lower back. Maybe we got along simply because we were all loser potheads.

"Lots of actors had 'em. They're all a lot more careful about it now." Rod said, proud of himself for finally catching out interest.

"You know who has a coke-nail?" Gerri spoke up.

"Who?" Rod asked after exhaling a mouthful of smoke. The grey tendrils hung in the stagnant air around us. It was the start of the summer and Rod's basement was barely air conditioned. We were all wearing tank-tops and shorts, and our hair was fuzzy with humidity.

"Travis." Gerri said.

"Stoker? Travis Stoker?"

She nodded.

"Dude, that guy is weird as hell." Rod shook his head and fingered his joint. It stank like a horned-up skunk, and I wished he'd pass it over to me. I reached out and took it after a few seconds. After taking in a lungful, I asked:

'Who's Travis Stoker?"

Rod bit his lower lip. "He graduated a few years back. Before our time."

"He lives across from me." Gerri said.

"Oh. That metalhead that sits on his porch in his boxers every morning?"

"Yeah. Him." Gerri nodded. "He's got a coke-nail. Which means…"

"He's got coke!" Rod exclaimed, as if we had just cracked a challenging code. I shook my head and passed the joint to Gerri.

"What do we need coke for when we got this dank?" I asked. I wasn't being sardonic either. I much preferred weed to the alternative intoxicants.

"Have you ever done coke before?" Gerri asked. "It'd really help with your ADHD, I think."

I sighed and looked at my watch. I had never done anything harder than weed. Well, except for shrooms at that rave we went to a year back… but it had made me shit my brains out the next day and that was no fun. "I'm not interested in coke." I said.

"Well, we should go score some then." Rod said.

"How much money do you have?" Gerri asked.

Rod shrugged, which meant he probably had twenty bucks at most. "How much does it cost?"

"I dunno." Gerri said. "The only time I did it was at a party, and I didn't pay for it."

"Maybe if you show him your tits, he'll give it to us for free." Rod was always talking about Gerri's tits. She laughed it off, but I knew he wanted to see them. I did too, so I won't judge. Gerri was curvy and beautiful, and I think she only hung out with us because she was a total geek when it came to her personality.

"That might work." She said, seriously considering it.

"How about it, Phil. You down?" Rod asked.

I shucked my shoulders and sucked in more weed. I really didn't want to do any coke, but if Gerri was going to pop her boobs out, I didn't want to miss it.

†

Our walk to Gerri's house was terrible. The sun beat down on us like we were lizards under a heat-lamp –I'm no writer, so these are the best metaphors you're gonna get outta me, you fuck. I think the last time I read a book for fun; it was a *Hank the Cowdog* story in the third grade.

I let my arms flop by my sides, and I watched Gerri as we went. She was a friend and I never really intended on asking her on a date, or even getting in her pants… but I was a horn-dog. I was always saving little details for the spank-bank. Rod was yammering on about some show he was watching on Disney+ and I just couldn't… give… a… shit… about Baby fuckin' Yoda. So, I watched the houses as we strolled by them. A few kids were lounging in a plastic pool. A tubby guy with white fur was mowing his lawn without a shirt. A girl around our age –we would have all been college freshman if we were pursuing an education after high-school, but that just wasn't in the cards-- was sunbathing on a lawn-chair and I took in a few peeks as we went by her. She didn't seem to notice me.

Gerri's house looked neat and trim. Her parents were total clean freaks. Across the way sat Travis Stoker's place. It was a dump. His windows were fogged over, his door was ratty, and his lawn was overgrown.

"He's a weird guy." Rod repeated.

"How so?" I asked.

"He doesn't really do anything. I've never seen him at a party or outside of his lawn. I don't even know where he works."

"He works at night." Gerri said. "I've seen him leave a few times."

"Okay. Okay. Who cares? Let's get the coke and go." I grumbled. I really didn't like being outside. Even Rod's basement was nicer than this. The air felt wet, and my lungs felt heavy. I really just wanted to get back on the sofa and watch more shitty *Star Wars* movies. I wanted to see Gerri's tits too but... I started to also think that there was no way that that would happen.

We walked up the porch and knocked on Travis's door. There was no answer.

Rod looked at his watch. "You said he only works at night, right?"

Gerri shrugged. "I mean, yeah but... I don't know his schedule."

Rod pounded on the door. Harshly. The racket made my chest clench up.

Suddenly, I could hear feet pounding toward the door. It swung open, and there Travis Stoker was. His face and belly were etched with tattoos and his eyes were baggy with weariness. He looked like he had just finished crying at a funeral. Except… one usually didn't go to funerals in the buff.

My face went red when I realized I was staring down at his massive cock, which was bobbing between his hairy thighs.

"What's up." Travis said, irritated. "What-the-fuck you want?"

"Uhm." Rod was looking at Travis's prick too. He seemed lost for words.

Gerri spoke up. "We wanted to see if we could score some coke off you."

Travis scratched at his eyelid with his left pinky. Indeed, he had a long, yellowed, and hooked fingernail. I looked at it, hoping it would distract me from his penis.

"What?" Travis burped.

"We... we thought you might have some cocaine." Rod stammered.

"How come?" Travis looked down the lawn and toward his mailbox. He seemed to be losing interest in us.

"Well," Rod continued, "you have..."

"You just seem cool and cool guys always have coke." Gerri interjected.

Travis smirked. "What you got for *me*, though?"

"We've got—" Gerri started.

"Money." As much as I wanted to see her boobs, I didn't want this creep looking at her. Especially since he lived right across the street. I didn't think I'd be able to sleep at night if he saw her naked. I'd imagine him lugging a ladder across the street and scuttling up to her bedroom window. Maybe he wouldn't have any clothes on then either.

And I wasn't lying. I had money. I never went out of the house without my wallet, which was currently stuffed with twenty --and ten-- dollar bills.

Travis shrugged. "A'ight. Come on." He vanished into his house.

And we followed him.

†

His house smelled. I mean, none of us were a bed of roses after our hike to Travis's house but... this place had a funk to it. It smelled like an unwashed ass. Like soiled toilet paper. Like vomit pooling in the bottom of a sick bucket. It smelled like an unbrushed mouth after recovering from influenza. I put a hand against my nose and pinched, not even caring if the motion insulted our host.

Gerri and Rod had better poker-faces than I did. They smiled toward Travis's back –and bare ass—as he walked into his living room and slumped into his sofa.

"Have a seat, guys." Travis said and indicated the floor beside his coffee-table. We squatted down, crossed our legs, and sat like children waiting for story time.

Travis hocked up a phlegm-ball and spat it onto the carpet. I suddenly felt self-conscious of my bare legs against the crusty flooring.

"So... coke, huh?" Travis asked.

"Yeah. Just… just enough for the two of us." Rod said. "Phil's staying sober."

I liked the idea of Travis knowing my name as well as I liked the idea of him creeping on Gerri in her sleep. My guts roiled and I squeezed my eyes shut. When I opened them, Travis was hefting himself up to his feet with monumental effort. He was as skinny as a toothbrush, but he seemed to struggle to carry around his own body. As if he was an inconvenience to himself. He stamped down the hall and vanished into one of his bedrooms. When he was out of earshot, I turned toward Gerri and said:

"We could run now before he gets back."

Gerri rolled her eyes. "We've made it this far."

"Yeah. Just imagine how we're gonna tell this story to our kids when it's all said-and-done." Rod snorted.

"I don't plan on telling my kids *any* stories about y'all." I laughed.

We broke into soft giggles. It made me feel better, knowing that this would all be over in a few moments, and we'd be—

Travis came running down the hallway. He hadn't put on clothes, but he was wearing a mask. It was a white, expressionless slate with two small, dark holes for his eyes. He had drawn roses on each cheek. They were crude drawings, but they were bright red, and each ended in a green tail. Gerri gasped, I froze, but Rod? He fucking screamed. When I realized that Travis was carrying a machete, I pulled in a breath for a scream myself. The noise died in my throat as Travis vaulted over the sofa and landed in front of Rod. He swung the machete down. It collided with a loud *thunk* on the top of Rod's dome. Blood exploded out from his fractured skull. It raced up the surface of the machete and gloved Travis's hands, dying them a deep and unforgiving red.

He jerked the machete free, and Rod flopped backward. His head collided with the wall and more blood shot out from the slit on the top of his head. His eyes rolled wildly in their sockets and his breaths came in with harsh hitches.

Gerri stood and raced toward the door, but Travis was after her. He wrapped a skinny arm around her throat and jerked backward. She fell to the ground and began to struggle.

And what was I doing while my best pal and my favorite girl were being abused? I sat in the crisscross-applesauce position and tried to decide which terrible thing I should be paying more attention to. Gerri's assault or Rod's death?

I looked back at Rod. His head was tilted toward his shoulder. A grey, wormy strand of brain matter oozed out from the fissure in his scalp. It drooled down his brow and fell into his lap. A huge, crimson bubble expanded from his left nostril. When it popped, I realized that it was his last breath.

I looked back at Gerri. Travis had hiked her shirt up. I could see Gerri's breasts, but I no longer wanted to. She was weeping as he palmed one of her breasts while holding the machete against her flexing throat. Blood oozed out from a thin red line beneath her chin. Her bucking and thrashing had resulted in several nicks and cuts. Travis was shushing her, squeezing her flesh hard. He was leaving white indentations along the surface of her breast. I was happy his right hand didn't have a coke-nail, since it could have easily torn her flesh open.

Travis looked up at me and jumped. He had forgotten I was there, apparently. He pressed the sharpened edge of the machete against Gerri's throat and said –in an unnaturally raspy tone: "You move... she dies."

I nodded, as if he needed confirmation that I understood. I could smell that Rod had soiled his drawers beside me.

Gerri looked toward me and mouthed: "Run." I couldn't obey her. I couldn't be responsible for her death. I already felt responsible for what Travis was doing to her breast. He was mulching it in his right hand. Squeezing and pulling and tearing...

"Stop." I muttered.

Travis waited for me to say more.

"Just... stop." I stated, more firmly. "I'll give you all my cash and... and I won't tell anyone."

Travis released Gerri's breast. I should have been relieved, but he put his free hand against the side of the machete's blade. It now lay across her throat like a guillotine.

I couldn't see Travis's face, but I could tell he was smiling.

He pushed all of his body weight into his arms. The decapitation was fast and clean. The skin rasped open, the esophagus crumpled in two, and blood hosed out from Gerri's neck stump. Her head thumped and rolled across the floor, landing beside the sofa's rounded front leg.

My mouth hung open and I watched in horror as Gerri's decapitated head *blinked*. Her mouth opened and closed, as if she was trying to speak. But Gerri wasn't capable of speech anymore. She was dead.

You didn't get to talk after you lost your head. Those are the rules.

I looked back at Travis just before he beat me across the head with the hilt of his blade.

†

When I woke up, I was naked in Travis's basement.

I wasn't alone. Rod was piled up in the left corner. He had been cut in half and his legs had been wrapped over his shoulders, like he was a piece of luggage and not a real person with feelings —who had loved *Star Wars* movies and weed. Across from me, Gerri was laid flat on her back. Her head was sitting on the mound of her pubis. She had had her clothes removed, but she was so blood spattered she didn't look naked.

I looked around. I was happy to realize that I wasn't restrained, and that Travis was nowhere to be seen. I looked up at the roof of the basement and was sad to see that the whole room had been soundproofed. The walls were thick, and the ceiling was padded. Even if I screamed, no one would do anything about it.

The ground was cold concrete. The blood from my best friends had solidified into an icy, red carpet.

"What's your name?" A voice called up from behind me.

I turned around.

She would have been pretty, if both her eyes hadn't been removed. She was tall, slender, and cherry-haired. Her skin was freckled and smooth, and her nakedness would have inspired me under better circumstances.

She was clearly another victim. I wondered what had brought her and Travis together. Maybe she had been hitchhiking, and he picked her up on his way home from the nightshift.

"I-I'm Phil." I said. "Phillipe Vazquez."

"Martha." She swallowed. I could hear her throat *crinkle*; it was so dry. Travis apparently didn't believe he needed to water his eye-less pet. Not that keeping us alive seemed like his ultimate goal.

"Are you okay?" It was a dumb question. Obviously, she wasn't okay. Neither of us were. But I didn't know what else to say.

She shivered before asking: "Do you still have your eyes?"

I nodded. Then, realizing she couldn't see my gesture, I said: "Yes."

"How about the others? I heard him drag two more in."

I looked back at Gerri's head. It was eyeless. Same with Rod. Both of my friends had had their eyeballs scooped out of their sockets and—

--and what? What had Travis done with the orbs?

"Where'd they go?" I asked.

Martha blanched. "I... I..."

I heard the basement door open. Heavy footsteps thumped down the stairs. Illuminated by the light from his kitchen, I could see Travis's figure. He was still naked, and masked. But he didn't have his machete, or any weapon that I could spy. I considered leaping toward him. I was certain I could take him, even though I wasn't very athletic. I spent most of my days getting high and working at a fast-food restaurant. My basketball days were long behind me.

I also didn't think I stood much of a chance against the killer. I would instinctively pull my punches. I would try and evade him rather than confront him. I wouldn't be much use in a fight.

How quickly one's spirit dies when facing true horror.

He clomped down the stairs and stopped at the last step. His masked face roved the room, as if he was observing all the carnage for the very first time. His eyes fell on me, and he rasped:

"Oh, good. You're awake."

"Please." I stammered. "Lemme go!"

"No." He answered swiftly. "Have you met Martha yet?" He indicated the blinded girl in the corner."

"Y-yes." I said.

"She's my fuck-doll." Travis said. "I almost made your gal-pal my newest toy but... I'm loyal to Martha. I wouldn't dream of letting some other skank off the street take her place. See, Martha knows... what I like."

Martha didn't object to his statements. She had gone mute. Maybe this was exactly what he liked. Servility and silence. Either way, I found myself suddenly thankful that Gerri had been spared this obscene fate.

"I'm not saying I didn't fuck your girl." Travis said. "I'm just saying... she was a dead lay." Travis laughed, and I hated him with every strand of my being.

I grimaced, clenched my teeth, and squinted. I wanted to look mean and tough, but I was no such thing.

Travis snickered and walked back up the stairs, leaving us in our solitude. Before snapping the door shut, he said: "You can fuck her too! Enjoy her while you can!"

I didn't take him up on the offer, although I could tell by her tense muscles and worried whimpers that Martha expected me to. I reassured her: "Hey, we're going to get out of here. I'm not going to hurt you, okay? We'll find a way out and—"

"There's no way out." Martha whispered. "No way."

I asked a very dark question: "How long have you been here?"

Martha turned her eyeless face up and frowned. "I don't know. Eight... nine... ten..." She paused. "Ten years?"

†

When Travis came back, I think a whole day had passed. I woke up to the wet suction noises of a penis sliding in and out of a moist hole. When I looked up from my cramped, fetal ball, I expected to see Travis raping Martha. And he was... but not in the way I had anticipated.

He was holding both sides of her head and thumping his bare pelvis back and forth against it. His cock was gliding into her left orbital socket. He had lubed it with spit, piss, and wound mucus. I could see a yellow, grey concoction leaking out of the hole and trailing down Martha's cheek like a diseased tear.

"Suck on my balls, bitch!" Travis commanded.

I couldn't see it, but I saw him shuffle around so that his scrotal sack filled her mouth. I imagined it tasted like sweat and dried paper. I imagined it made her uvula tremble and her tongue curl.

Martha grunted but didn't scream or cry. Apparently, she was used to this vile intrusion.

Travis didn't pull out when he came. Instead, he pushed his hips into her face and squirted cum down her eye-shaft. When he did dislodge his penis from her crater, there was a creamy, white fluid leaking freely from the hole. She fell back onto her rump and mutedly tipped her head forward. It didn't totally flush out the sex-fluids, but a few strands of cum drained out of the hole and pattered against the ground between her spread legs.

Travis jerked his deflating cock a few times, squeezing out the last drops of his rancid seed. Then he turned his masked head toward me and said:

"That was a good 'un!"

I wanted to throw up.

†

He came up to me the next day and asked if I was thirsty. I couldn't lie. I was parched. I nodded and cried, and he held his dick out and told me to open wide. I'd never been pissed on before, even in my kinkiest sexual encounters. His piss tasted sour, and fumes seem to rise from his spray. After he had filled my mouth, he clamped it and my nose closed and told me I had to swallow. If I didn't, then he'd kill me. I almost wanted him to, but I swallowed anyways.

When I'd finished coughing, he said this: "Now, I gave you a little something... I think it's about high time you gave me a bit o' something in return."

I looked up sheepishly. I couldn't see his face, but I imagined he was licking his lips.

He held up his left hand and brandished his pinky finger. "This is why y'all thought I had coke, wasn't it? You thought this was a coke-finger?"

I couldn't deny him the truth. I nodded. He responded with a creaky laugh.

"You wish." He muttered.

And I did. I wish we had just scored some coke and did it in Rod's basement. I wished we were just spending another lazy day down there, watching garbage, smoking weed, and accomplishing nothing with our lives. Lethargy was better than torment. I'd have taken a non-event of a life over a trauma like this.

"You wanna know what I use this nail fer?" Travis asked. I shook my head, but he told me anyways: "*Scoopin'*."

He took me by the throat and pinned me to the ground. Unfed, terrified, and achy from a lack of sleep, I could barely fight back. He put his knees against my arms and lowered his pelvis onto my breastbone. He nestled in and used his right hand to hold my head steady.

When his pinky extended and inched toward my right eye, I suddenly developed the will to fight. My legs kicked, my fists clenched, and I began to bare my teeth. I roared and cried and panted, but I could do nothing to stop it. He fit the hooked tip of the pinky-nail between my eyeball and the bridge of my nose. I felt the eyeball well up with wet pain. Tears jetted out from the orb, as did a milky fluid. He had punctured the ball already! The serrated and unclean edges of the nail had cut along the side of the ocular organ, and now my socket was filling with clear juices.

"No!" I hollered. "No!"

Travis ignored my objections. He began to wiggle his finger back and forth, exhuming my right eye in slow strokes. I could feel it bulge in place before it popped free. Then, the quickly deflating sac rested against my cheek… and I could taste the salty interior waters of my eye as they filled my nostril and oozed into my sputtering lips.

Before I could even recognize that I was blinded on one side, he quickly got to work on the other eye.

In no time at all, I could see nothing.

Nothing at all.

But I could hear him.

He ate both of my eyes. He popped them into his mouth, sucked on them, and groaned with joy as he squeezed them between his rotten teeth.

"I can't see. I can't see." I repeated it over and over again, more to myself than to my captor. I said it all night, even when he was gone, and it was just me and Martha… alone in the permanent darkness.

†

That night, I was in so much pain, I didn't even realize Martha was touching me until her mouth grazed my inner thigh. I leapt backward and collided with the wall.

"Who is that?" I roared.

"Shhh." Martha said.

"Don't hurt me!" I honked.

"I'm not gonna hurt you." Martha reassured me. "Shhh. It's okay. It's okay, baby." She put her arms around me and pulled me in close. I began to weep against her chest. She smelled like sulfur; she was so unwashed. I could taste body-grease and dried sweat fill my mouth when I sucked in her aromas. She was comforting me, but all she did was remind me of where I was. Of what had become of me.

"It's okay." Martha said. "I just… wanna know what it's like with someone else."

"What?" I asked.

"He ain't never brought a live one before." Martha said. "And… and I've only ever been with *him*."

What was she saying? That he had stolen her virginity as well as her life? That she was consenting to sex with me since I was –to her—the last man left on the planet that wasn't her tormentor? It was wrong. It was all wrong. Neither of us should have been put in this scenario. And yet… here we were, and her graceless hand was fumbling for my naked prick. I could feel it grow against her hand; my body relieved to have something to focus on other than the pain in my sockets

"What are you doing?" I asked.

"Shhh." She repeated and began to kiss my chest.

I felt my heart leap into my throat. I melted in her hands.

She kissed my cock. Gingerly and delicately. She had known nothing but violence for ten years, and yet she didn't seem capable of committing it. I was comforted by her tenderness.

Until she began to work my heavy erection into her socket. I could tell that's what it was, because it didn't have teeth or a tongue. It was just a dry, unhealed hole. She began to work her head up and down my shaft and I screamed!

I pushed her away and heard her thump against the floor. She suddenly shouted: "Wait!"

I got on top of her and grabbed her by the sides of her head.

"Wait!" She hollered. "That's just how it's done! That's how it's always don—"

I lifted her head and smashed it against the floor. The concrete punched the back of her skull in instantly. I could hear a ripple of blood cascade from her broken head. I lifted it and slammed it into the floor once again, causing her to gargle –like she was using mouthwash, only it was blood that spumed out from between her clenched teeth. I hit her head against the floor repeatedly. I don't know what she wound up looking like… but she felt like a rotten cantaloupe in my hands by the time I was satisfied.

†

I wish I could tell you why I killed Martha. She didn't deserve it, that's for sure. Maybe I just thought it was more merciful that I do it, rather than allow her to live out more torments from our captor.

I'm waiting now for Travis to return. The basement is quiet except for the dribble of blood leaking from Martha's skull. I've been writing my story in my head, and if I ever get out of this basement, then maybe I'll tell it to someone, and they can put it on paper.

Maybe.

But for now, I'm just waiting. I'm waiting for Travis to come down and see what I did. Maybe he'll be so mad, he kills me on the spot. Maybe he'll make me take Martha's place.

Maybe he'll cry.

Maybe he'll laugh.

If I get out of here alive... I'll let you know.

SOMETHING AKIN TO REVULSION

Something about Jace Burton really got to Kayla Grace.

Maybe it was her lopsided smile, or the way she picked at her fingernails in class, or the fact that she had two pimples sat on her right cheek, or maybe it was that she didn't seem interested in making friends. Whatever it was, it filled Kayla with something akin to revulsion. A dense cloud of hatred polluted her veins and gripped her stomach with internal agony. Every time Kayla saw Jace Burton, she just wished that the bitch would *die*.

Kayla had never thought to call anyone a 'bitch' before. The word felt unnatural in her mouth and in her head. She was, after all, only eleven. But when she saw Jace, it was the only word she could think.

And wishing death on someone? It was a foreign notion to her. Kayla went to Sunday school. She read her Bible every night before bed, and she believed in prayer. She knew that it was a sin to wish death on anyone. But would it really count as a sin if it was someone so easy to hate? Even if there was no definite reason why they were so easy to hate?

Maybe God had invented Jace to test Kayla. Maybe if Kayla did nothing to her, then she'd be rewarded with a special ticket to Heaven. No waiting in line outside the pearly gates, no evaluation of sins, and no stern meetings with St. Peter necessary! Just one, two, three and off to the races!

But God had also created mosquitos and wood-ticks, and Kayla was certain that they had been mistakes. So, maybe that's all Jace was. A mistake.

Maybe, if Kayla did something about Jace... God would be happy that Kayla cleaned up his mess and spared him the trouble.

Kayla walked up to Jace at recess that day and said: "Hey. What are you doing after school?"

Jace looked shocked. She should have been. Kayla was one of the most popular girls in the sixth grade. She was tall, blonde, and freckled. Everyone doted on her, and all the boys had crushes on her. This last Valentine's Day, her desk had been so stuffed with cards she had had to throw a few out just to make room for more.

Jace, on the other hand, was portly, small, and looked about three years younger than she actually was. Her knees were so scabby, they looked like the resting places of a colony of dried-up ladybugs.

"I... I don't know." Jace said. "Nuthin', I guess."

"You wanna go to the creek with me and some of my pals?"

"I... uhm... sure!" Jace smiled. Her face went red, and her eyes were as wide as saucers. She looked like she was about to be squished by a steamroller.

"Cool. Meet in the playground after school, yeah?"

"O-Okay." Jace said.

When Kayla went back to her circle of friends, Lucy asked: 'What did you say to freak-o-zoid?"

"I told her to come to the creek with us today." Jace said.

"Get real!" Ruth retorted.

"Are you trying to get on Santa's good-list?" Terri chided.

"Nah." Kayla shrugged and looked from one face to the other. Her friends were all like her. Prematurely stern and hopelessly popular. They all had long hair, stick-like bodies, and manicured nails. Lucy was the tallest, Ruth was the smallest, and Terri was the only one that wasn't blonde. Her short, black hair was cut to the nape of her neck.

"What are we gonna do with her? Push her in?" Ruth asked.

"No. We should tie her to a tree and leave her there!" Terri offered.

"No." Kayla cut in. "I have a way, way better idea."

†

The walk to the creek was quick. They met Jace in the playground and carted her across the football field and toward the woods. The football team was doing drills, but none of the high school kids took notice of the girls. It was windy and blustery, but not yet cold. Kayla bit her lower lip and said:

"Have you been out to the creek before?"

Jace shook her head. "No. But, I hear all the cool kids go out there." She blushed, knowing how awful that sounded. "Like, you guys and… and everyone else."

"Well, we'll initiate you! That way, you're cool too!" Kayla said.

"Oh, I don't think she can handle the initiation!" Terri quipped. "She doesn't have the guts for it!" She poked Jace in the stomach, as if they were familiar enough to touch each other. Jace looked uncomfortable, but she said nothing.

"Crap-ola. She's got plenty of guts!" Lucy took her turn, pressing Jace's belly and laughing.

Reel it in, guys. Kayla said through a telepathic glare. *We don't want her running home to Mama just yet.*

They walked Jace up and over a row of dimpled hills, then down a steep slope. At the bottom of the slope stood a tight row of trees. The forest stretched on for miles behind the school, and only a few kids were brave enough to crawl through it and to the creek. It was easy to get lost in all those trees, bushes, and shrubs.

The earth crackled beneath their shoes as they marched Jace into the woods and around a well-trodden path. Before long, they were at the creek. It was only a trickle today, but sometimes it rushed with force! It wasn't a great place for swimming, but you could wade in and cool your toes on hot days! And everyone loved a good splash from a well-meaning friend! The real object of attraction was the flat rock that rested beside the creek. It was wide, long, and smooth, and was perfect for a group of girls to sit on for a gab session.

"Wow!" Jace exclaimed upon seeing the rock.

They all climbed up onto it and lounged like warm reptiles.

Kayla put her hands beneath her head and sighed contentedly.

"So, do you guys come down here every day?" Jace asked.

"No. Just every now and again." Lucy answered.

"It's so relaxing. I love it!"

"Well, you don't get to relax just yet." Terri said. "You haven't been initiated yet!"

"W-what's that mean?" Jace asked.

"You don't know what the word 'initiation' means?" Ruth piped in.

"It means, if you want to join us you have to earn it." Kayla said.

Jace's face fell. She looked like someone had just cracked an egg over her head.

"Don't worry." Terri said. "It's not that bad. You just gotta do this one thing and then you can be a part of our group... forever."

"Really?" Jace asked.

"Yeah. We'll be BFF's!" Terri continued, laying it on a bit thick.

"You gotta be brave though." Kayla said, still keeping her eyes closed and her head relaxed.

"What is it? I'll do it for sure!" Jace said with a smile. She was bolstered by Terri's encouragement, it seemed.

"You gotta retrieve something for us." Kayla said.

"What?" Jace asked.

Kayla drew out the suspense. "Nothing special."

"What is it?"

Everyone waited with bated breath before Kayla said: "Just a rock."

"This one." Lucy said, fishing a stone up from the creek. It was palm-sized, round, and knobby.

"What?" Jace asked.

"Yeah. Lucy will drop it… and all you need to do is get it and bring it back here. Then, you're one of us!" Ruth said.

"We've all done it." Kayla lied. This was the first time this ritual was taking place.

"Well, that sounds easy." Jace smirked.

"Okay. Let's do it then." Kayla hopped up to her feet, strolled away from the sitting stone, and led the way into the woods.

Jace followed, and the rest of the girls took up the rear. They walked through the underbrush and up a hill, far enough so that the creeks gentle trickle was muted.

Kayla could only hope that Jace's heart had stopped in her chest when she spied the tunnel.

The shaft had once been the entrance to a mine, a long, long time ago. Multiple holes like this one dotted the hills, but very few of them had survived the weather. There were floods too, and this mine shaft had filled with dense, cloudy water. It was just a little pool in the woods now, but Kayla knew that this pool stretched on and on forever.

Confidently, she chucked the rock into the pool. It sank from sight, leaving nothing more than a ripple.

Jace hesitated. "Wait." She said. "I'm not... I'm not going in there."

"I thought you said you wanted to be a part of our gang?" Ruth asked, sounding genuinely confused.

"Yeah, but... but..." Jace looked from one girl to the other, hoping for reason. There was none to be found. They all wore confused expressions and frowns.

"We all did it before." Terri said. "It's honestly not that bad. Just a little swim and then you're at the bottom. And if you swim forward, it opens up into a really cool cavern!" This was all, of course, a lie.

"But... but..."

"You sure do like butts, don't you?" Lucy said with a snide chuckle.

"C'mon, kid." Kayla nudged Jace's shoulder. "You can do it. Just jump in, get the rock, and jump out. It's not hard at all. It's easy."

Jace crossed her arms and shook her head. "What if there are snakes in there?"

Terri guffawed.

"Really, we've all done it before. You're making a big deal out of nothing." Ruth said.

"I told you she'd chicken out." Lucy sighed.

"Come on, Jace!" Terri honked.

"Really, we'll be right here." Kayla said, trying to sound like a big sister. "Just go in... come out... and we'll all go back to the stone, and we'll lay out to dry."

"O-okay." Jace muttered. She stepped toward the pool. It was narrow. About as wide as she was. "B-but you promise it'll be okay, right?"

"We promise." Terri said.

"Cross our hearts."

Jace pulled off her skirt and shirt, held her nose, sucked in a deep breath, and jumped in. The moment she was beneath the water... the other girls ran.

†

Back at Kayla's house, the girls all laughed themselves hoarse. They imagined how frightened Jace would be when she came back to the surface and found herself all alone. Worse yet, Terri had been bright enough to scoop up Jace's clothes and take them with her. She had dumped the garments into the creek. Jace would have to pry them out from between two stones and lay them out to dry on the rock. How embarrassed she would be! Kayla was certain that

Jace would be too humiliated by the prank to tattle, but she was also sure they could convince everyone she was lying for attention if she did happen to tell. Besides, Jace was a nobody. It would be her word against theirs, and the words of Kayla, Lucy, Ruth, and Terri bore a lot more weight than Jace could muster.

"She'll probably cry when she sees us at school on Monday." Ruth said with a giggle.

"She has the whole weekend to get over it." Kayla shrugged. "She'll probably just ignore us."

"I wish we could've seen her face when she came back up for air!" Lucy crowed.

"That was such a good idea, Terri. Really." Ruth said.

"Terri? It was my idea!" Kayla hissed.

"Sorry. Kayla." Ruth corrected herself.

Terri blanched.

"It's going to be so funny when we see her again." Ruth continued.

†

The next day, Kayla heard her parents talking at the dinner table. Apparently, a young girl had gone missing the day prior, and the police were on the lookout for her.

"Hon, do you know a Jace Burton?" Her mom asked as she tried to pour her morning cereal without trembling.

"Who?" Kayla asked, knowing her face was scarlet.

"She may be a classmate of yours I think." Her mother said. "God, I hope she turns up. Her poor mother must be terrified."

"Burton?" Her father said. "Oh, Christ. I know her dad."

"R-Really?" Kayla asked.

Her father nodded slowly.

The family ate breakfast in silence.

†

By Monday, search teams were looking through the woods for Jace's body. When her clothes were discovered crumpled up in a creek, the news showed a video of her mother and father weeping over her stained, tattered, and wettened shirt. Everyone was feeling grim, but no one seemed to have remembered seeing Kayla, Lucy, Ruth, or Terri walking with

Jace into the very woods where her clothing was found. As far as Kayla knew, Jace hadn't told anyone where she was going either.

She bit into her tongue and wondered why she hadn't cried. Kayla was scared, of course. She could hardly sleep. But she wasn't worried for Jace or her family. Instead, she wondered what would happen if she was caught. Would she be crucified by the townspeople? Would she be branded a murderer?

She was certain that Jace was dead. She knew it…

She invited her friends over for a sleepover. Their parents were reluctant given the terrible news that had shocked their small town, but after a while… they were convinced that their little girls needed to be around their friends to feel safe. And so, in Kayla's room, the four girls spoke in whispers:

"What do we do?" Lucy asked. "I mean, do we tell someone?"

"No!" Terri rasped.

"I mean, not about *us*. We could like, call in an anonymous tip. Let them know to search that flooded mine-shaft."

"She probably drowned." Ruth muttered. "Oh, God. We ran off and she probably drowned."

"I don't know." Kayla shook her head. "I mean, how? What could have happened to her under there?"

"Maybe she followed Terri's dumb advice and went looking for that made-up underground cavern... and got lost." Lucy accused.

"Hey! Don't blame me! We all convinced her to go in."

"Shush!" Kayla said. 'What if my folks hear you?"

"Sorry. I just... don't blame me. This wasn't my fault." She screwed up her face. "It was your idea anyways, Kayla."

"Shut up." Kayla snarled.

"No, really... it was your idea. Why should we *all* feel guilty? You, like, manipulated us into going along with it."

"You all agreed to do it." Kayla said, on the defensive.

"Whatever." Ruth said and stood. "I just think it's terrible. All of it. All of us. We should do... *something*."

"Like what?" Kayla snapped.

"Like... what Lucy said. An anonymous call. Let them know where to look for her... her body."

"We didn't kill her." Kayla said. "It was just a joke. She got her-own-dumb-self drowned." Kayla crossed her arms. "I don't see why we have to do anything for her."

There was a knock on the bedroom door. The girls all turned their heads and watched as it inched open. Kayla could hear everyone's heart thudding in their chests.

Her mother poked her head in: "Girls, its almost bedtime. Remember, you all have school tomorrow."

"Sure thing, Mrs. G. G'night!" Terri waved.

†

Kayla lay snuggled beside her teddy bear while her friends snoozed in their sleeping bags on the floor. She was struggling to sleep. Her mind kept crawling back to that cloudy pool. She had dreams that were more like jump-scares. She imagined looking into the pool and seeing Jace's bloated corpse floating just beneath the surface. Wadded up like a ball of tissue paper, made from human meat. Her eyes bugging out of her skull as if they were going to pop out of it and—

Kayla stood and carefully tiptoed toward her bedroom door. Confident she hadn't woken her friends; she went into the hall and into the bathroom. She closed the door politely, turned on the sink, brushed her hair away from her freckled face, then knelt over the toilet and threw up. After she finished yakking up her dinner, she shut the sink off and brushed her teeth almost diligently. Then, she sat on the closed toilet lid, buried her face into her palms, and wept.

When she went back to her room, she was happy to see she hadn't disturbed her friend's sleep. She walked across the room, nestled back into bed, and looked over the lumps that lay across her floor.

Terri was just by the foot of the bed.

Lucy was beside it.

Ruth was near the door.

And...

And...

Who was that by the closet?

Kayla felt her heart crank up its pace. Her mouth went dry, and her eyes began to flutter. She sad upright and blinked, hoping that the slumped shape lying on the ground by the closet was just a figment of her imagination. She hoped it would vanish, or at least be revealed to be something other than a human body.

But it was moving. Its breath was wet and noisy, and its body moved so sluggishly it looked like an oversized maggot in the darkness.

Oh, God. Oh, God. Is this real? Is this real?

Kayla reached for her nightstand and flicked on the lamp.

It revealed the corpses of her friends.

Of course, Kayla hadn't woken them up when she had crawled out of her room. They had been dead for a long time. Each girl had been killed in their sleeping bags, and they had been killed without a sound.

A plastic bag was wrapped around each head. They were wrinkled and indented, especially where they had been pulled into the mouths by each girl's frantic breaths.

Kayla looked from one body to the next, her heart iced over with panic.

She looked back up and toward the intruder.

She had expected it to be Jace. Instead, she was surprised to see a full-grown woman. Tall, gaunt, and haggard. Her eyes were weeping with tears, her face was etched with misery, and her hair was stringy and black. She was wearing rubber dish gloves, and a jacket.

The woman grinned. It was such an awful sight, her wide-toothed smile. Kayla could feel her bed instantly dampen with panicked sweat.

"P-please." Kayla said.

The woman stood. She was six-feet tall. Her head tilted to the side and her grin persisted. Kayla saw that she was holding a knife. It gleamed in the low light of Kayla's room.

Kayla wanted to scream as the woman approached, but no sounds came from her trembling mouth. Instead, she listened as the woman said:

"My lil sister came home… cold… shiverin'… she tolt me whut you did."

The woman was speaking in a whisper, as if she was in a library. Her smile never wavered, even as she drew closer and closer to Kayla.

"She told me you played a trick on her. Well, I decided... to play a trick on *you*."

"Please." Kayla stammered.

"Jace is hiding out in my apartment right now. She's fine and safe... but she's hurt. Real hurt. And I don't let nobody hurt my baby sister."

The woman grabbed Kayla by the throat, squeezing off her scream before she could unleash it.

"Ain't... nobody... hurts... my... sister..." The woman grinned as she slammed the knife into Kayla's face.

Kayla felt her flesh split open and watched as blood splashed across the front of the woman's jacket. When the knife was pulled loose, it came free with a wet *sucking* noise, as if her skin was trying to pull the blade back into place.

The woman released Kayla. She fell back onto her bed and shuddered with pain. Blood flew up from the fissure beside her left eye. She shook and rattled in place.

The woman began to stab her chest. The knife heaved in and out of Kayla with rapid bites. More blood filled the air. It drenched the corpses of Kayla's friends. It leaked into the mattress and spilled out from beneath the bed itself. It dusted the walls and left little dots on the window.

The woman left the knife buried in Kayla's chest. Her breath sounded like a short burp now. Kayla's eyes had even gone red.

She watched as the smiling woman admired her handiwork. Each cut was, to this crazy woman, a work of art. Then, she reached into the pocket of her jacket and pulled loose a small object.

"Jace wanted you to have this." The smiling woman said. "I don't know why. But she said, before I left to do this, that it was... important."

The smiling woman showed Kayla the small, knobby, rounded stone that Jace had retrieved from the pool. The mere sight of it caused Kayla to tremor with guilt, fear, and repulsion all at once.

"No..." Kayla wheezed through her broken mouth. "No... no... no..."

The smiling woman got to work, finishing the task she had come here to complete. With a deft touch, she pried Kayla's mouth open, and screwed the stone in place atop her tongue. She then pulled out a pouch from the inner pockets of her jacket. Quietly and quickly, she sewed Kayla's mouth shut. As the needle wound up and through Kayla's lips, she swallowed hard. The stone was lodged in her mouth but was too big to fall down her throat. As she bled out and died, Kayla wondered what the police would think when they undid her stitches and found the stone planted in her jaw.

She could only hope that her death would make one hell of a story for the town to speculate over.

The smiling woman pulled the knife out of Kayla's chest and used it to cut the twine.

"There." She said as she admired the corpse. "All done."

SOMETHING AKIN TO REVULSION

AFTERWORD (STORY NOTES)

Telling a story to an audience is an exciting and nerve-wracking thing. I love the thrill of it, which is why I'd say I'm addicted to writing. I do it every day. I crave it when I'm at work, or when I wake up in the middle of the night after a bad dream. It consumes me.

Which is, of course, why I think its always a good idea for authors to offer some insight into what brought their stories to life. I'd rather tell you how each story was conceived rather than leave you in the dark...

So, here we go...

LOLCOW:

I read this one for the Gross Out Contest at Killercon '22. If you've never been to a Gross Out, I highly recommend it. Basically, each contestant tries to capture the audience's attention in a limited amount of time. Halfway through, an emcee stops the reading and asks if the audience wants the reader to finish their story. Reading this story to a full audience, being judged by genre heavyweights Wrath James White, John Skipp, and Shane McKenzie? With Jeff Strand emceeing? Holy shit, talk about a wild ride. And I truly didn't expect to win because every story before and after mine was totally disgusting.

The story itself came from my loose interest in the darker side of internet culture. Sometimes, I fall down the rabbit hole and watch 'cringe comps', video essays on internet drama, and LolCow's. It's like a car crash you can't look away from. It's sometimes shocking, heartbreaking, and always embarrassing.

LIQUID SICK:

I'm a trans woman. If you didn't know that about me, hello. I'm very trans and very gay. And so, in the last few years the rise of TERF ideologies have really upset and concerned me. Writing this story was very cathartic.

REHEARSAL:

My novella *Your God Can't Save You* had many starts and stops before it took the form it ultimately became. This was one of them. A violent call-out story that showed a self-righteous rapist leading a band of deviants into his school with guns. This was the prologue. I think it was the only part of that version of the story that worked. I edited it so that it felt like one complete story with an open ending, and more of a *House on the Edge of the Park* vibe. Its really just a mean story about bad people doing horrible things. There's no morals, resolution, or hope.

BODY-CRUNCH:

This was another one that started as a larger story. It was set up to be *Of Mice and Men* but make it extreme... and it did not work. But I loved the backwoods wrestling-ring sequence, so I took that part and made it into its own story. A lot of short stories do start as longer works, and a lot of longer works sometimes begin as short stories! Writing is just like that sometimes.

COKE-NAIL:

I've always been oddly fascinated by coke-nails... and I also always wondered if anyone accidentally scratched their own eye out with one. That idea kind of morphed into something resembling a slasher... mixed with a torture-porn flick from the early oo's. I find this story really bleak, which is why I chose to give it a more ambiguous ending. I do hope Phil makes it out of Travis's basement someday...

SOMETHING AKIN TO REVULSION:

Maybe not the goriest story I've ever written, but I was going for mor emotional brutality than gross-out gags with this one. I think it's a pretty decent palate cleanser after everything that came before it, don't you?

I mapped out three potential endings and then went with the one that felt right by the time I actually wrote the damn thing. In one alternate universe, Jace's zombified corpse comes up and bludgeons the girls with the stone. In another, Kayla's guilt crushes her, and she winds up killing her friends in an attempt to avenge the girl she was responsible for abusing. But I'm way, way happier with the 'Big Sister' ending. It was a neat challenge to write something 'creepier' rather than straight-up disgusting. Don't expect too many chillers from me in the future but... I hope you enjoyed this one.

So, there we have it! Six stories to frighten, alarm, and repulse you. I hope you had fun reading these! If you did, be sure to leave a review on Amazon or Goodreads! Post about the book on Facebook, Tik-Tok, Instagram... wherever you'd like! Indie horror relies on you, dear reader, to thrive!

With love,
JUDITH SONNET

Printed in Great Britain
by Amazon